BEG ME

JESSA JAMES

GET A FREE BOOK!

Join my mailing list to be the first to know of new releases, free books, special prices and other author giveaways.

http://freehotcontemporary.com

Beg Me: Copyright © 2018 by Jessa James

All Rights Reserved. No part of this book may be reproduced or transmitted in any form or by any means, electrical, digital or mechanical including but not limited to photocopying, recording, scanning or by any type of data storage and retrieval system without express, written permission from the author.

Published by Jessa James
James, Jessa
Beg Me

Cover design copyright 2018 by Jessa James, Author
Images/Photo Credit: Deposit Photos: konradbak

Publisher's Note:
This book was written for an adult audience. The book may contain explicit sexual content. Sexual activities included in this book are strictly fantasies intended for adults and any activities or risks taken by fictional characters within the story are neither endorsed nor encouraged by the author or publisher.

This book was previously published.

ABOUT BEG ME:

Lucas Ferris isn't like my brother's other business associates. He's sex on a stick. Six foot four with inky black hair. He smolders when he looks at me. My stepbrother made a deal, and Lucas comes to collect. My brother underestimates me. As for Mr Ferris, well, heís doing things to my body I never thought I wanted but crave so much.

If youíre looking for a panty-melting read with a hot as hell male, a feisty female, and a twist you wonít see coming, read on!

Note: This is a super sexy, steamy romance that will make your cheeks burn and your panties melt! Guaranteed HEA.

CHAPTER 1

"Why are we here Aiden? This is our family cabin, where we shared memories with Mom and Dad, not a place for business deals." She asked standing in the doorway getting ready to leave and go for a swim.

Her step-brother gave her a scolded look as he passed by and entered the foyer of the multi-million dollar cabin. "I don't want to have to tell you again Reagan. You know damn well why we're here. This is the biggest deal of my fucking life, our life and I have to seal it. You will fucking play your part... no questions asked! Do you understand?"

Her eyes fell to the floor to avoid eye contact with his angry eyes. She hated being a pawn in all of her brother's business deals. Being used like a commodity but in the end, she always went along with it. She walked into the living room that was floor to ceiling windows and looked out at the beautiful lake below.

Reagan Kade didn't normally make practice of lusting after her big brother's business associates. In fact, to her brother, they were supposed to be lusting after her while he herded them into signing his business deals. It was a partnership between the two that started only a year ago.

"Rule number one, always make the best use of your assets,

Reagan," her brother would tell her. 'Her assets' meant her looks and her body. Something she didn't lack. She had lush curves and ample breasts, which always drew the eye of both male and females. She could have easily passed for a runway model with her flawless and stunning looks. When her brother's associates were busy ogling her perky tits, they always lost concentration on the business at hand. At first, it hadn't been like that. Aiden had always requested that she be present while he conducted business but when she grew tired of it, Reagan expressed that she wasn't going to be his toy anymore, that is until the night he sat her down and gave her an ultimatum. It was either she be their distraction or she was cut out of the family business that he now controlled. That was an easy decision overall and it wasn't hurting anything or anyone as long as there was no physical contact. Unfortunately, she didn't have a choice.

This weekend though was different. Normally they would stay at their family mansion located in La Jolla, California but when Aiden told her they were flying out to Lake Tahoe to stay at the family cabin, it raised suspicion. The cabin wasn't a place for business negotiations; it was a place of family memories. But, Lucas Ferris had come to stay with them for the weekend and talk business so Reagan agreed to play hostess. Her brother Aiden had also made a huge fuss about her wardrobe and picked out certain outfits that she would wear for the weekend which was completely out of the norm.

She didn't argue, though. When her mother, Carey remarried she was only ten and Reagan loved her new family, specifically her big brother who was twelve years older than her. Aiden and her new step-father, Sean had always treated her like blood right from the beginning but when they were both killed in a car accident eighteen months ago Reagan was crushed and terrified. She had already lost her biological father when she was a toddler and now she only had her older step brother to care for her which wouldn't be an issue financially because Aiden had inherited his father's multi-million dollar land developer company. Reagan's biggest fear was to be alone, no family and she swore to god that would not happen.

As she had looked over at Mr. Ferris earlier in the day she noticed he wasn't like the other business men her brother usually invited to their house. His usual business associates were older, pot-bellied and ready to keel over or at least had one foot in the grave, but Ferris didn't look a day over thirty. Okay, maybe thirty-five. She had met him a few times previous in her California home. He was extremely fit and muscular and had inky black hair just long enough that you could run your hands through. He looked to be at least six foot four and had a smoldering intense sex on a stick type of look. Handsome didn't justify his looks at all with that deep-skin tan and smoldering deep-set eyes that were dark orbs of blue.

She found it to be strange, he didn't look like he was here for business at all and who the hell brings a bodyguard with them? The guy looked like a huge gorilla standing outside on guard for Christ sakes. She had been watching him since they had arrived and neither he nor her brother had talked over one business deal or looked at one shred of paper. She just shrugged it off.

The beautiful day had turned into night and she noticed that Mr. Ferris seemed to be watching her too. Sometimes it felt like he was devouring her with his eyes and she couldn't help herself. When she turned to check, she noticed he made no effort to hide the fact that he was checking her out. Every inch of her. A devilish grin would pull at his lips and he would give her a slight nod of his head. Reagan found it flattering, yet at the same time disturbing and strange.

After a late dinner, they moved into the family room and her brother and Mr. Ferris sat and exchanged light talk, while Reagan made them another round of drinks behind the wet bar. Her eyes would frequently look out at the two men, pretending to be in her game mode, but she was utterly exhausted and only wanted to go to bed. She gave the men their drinks and returned to a bar stool admiring Mr. Ferris's physique as he stood and stretched. Her eyes trailed to his broad shoulders and then up to his thick neck. When her eyes wandered up to his face, she was shocked to see the intensity in his eyes as he returned her stare. He looked like an animal ready to attack his prey and then a second later the look was gone like it was never there and replaced with a genuine smile. It made Reagan's heart race and she suddenly felt incredibly uncomfortable.

Reagan turned in her stool to avoid his contact. What the hell was wrong with her? She was used to men staring at her but that look, Lucas' look was different. Almost predatory and it frightened her. She was still a virgin and had just turned nineteen last week. She wasn't very familiar with sexual feelings; oh she had her share of college guys she had dated but she knew that they either wanted her because of her money or body and she sure as hell wasn't about to hand her virginity over to some frat boy that had no idea what he was doing. Nope! She was saving herself for the right man. A man that wanted her for her and nothing more. She wanted her first time to be magical and a night to remember for the rest of her life. That wasn't so much to ask for she thought.

A few minutes passed by and as she turned to look at her brother and guest a yawn escaped and she couldn't help but apologize as they both looked at her.

Aiden smiled and said, "It's been a long day sis. Why don't you head to bed and we'll see you in the morning."

"Are you sure?" She asked raising an eyebrow and stepping off the stool. She watched Lucas stand. "Aiden's right. Go get some sleep while we exchange boring banter. Tomorrow is another day." He said giving her a sly wink.

She turned to start walking up the large cedar staircase and stopped, turning to them, smiling. "Goodnight. I'll see you both in the morning for breakfast." As she began walking, she heard Mr. Ferris say, "Sleep well."

When she reached the landing she headed down the hall to her room. She closed the door and shedded her clothing and slipped into only a t-shirt and kept her panties on. After spending most of the day swimming and in the sun, she was utterly exhausted. Only two days to go and this will all be over she thought to herself. She climbed into bed and covered herself up to her waist with the bedsheet and slipped into a deep sleep.

CHAPTER 2

*L*ucas made his way up the stairs at two thirty in the morning and walked down the hall carrying a small satchel on his left shoulder. When he reached Reagan's room he turned to his bodyguard that hovered over him and whispered. "No one comes in."

"Yes, sir," Frankie said and nodded to his employer.

Lucas quietly opened the door to Reagan's room and eased his way in slowly shutting the door behind him. His eyes took in the surroundings as the moonlight flooded through the window giving him the perfect amount of light to see and move around freely.

He took a step to the edge of the bed as the light from the window illuminated Reagan's beautiful figure lying on the bed. He could see she was in a very deep sleep and he didn't want to wake her. Not yet. She was lying on the right side of the four-poster California king bed, her arms spread out across the pillows. His eyes trailed her lush body that was concealed beneath the thin sheet and her silky long strawberry blonde hair was fanned out on the pillow. He felt his cock swell as he imagined what it was going to feel like when he gripped her hair with his fists.

He licked his lips in anticipation. Not yet, he told himself.

He opened the small satchel that he was carrying and attached a special restraint to each of the four bedposts. Each soft casing held a mechanism that allowed him to have control of his prisoner's range of movement by increasing and decreasing the amount of slack in the cable. A devilish grin splayed across his face as he carefully removed the thin sheet that was covering her torso and legs. Not one sound or movement came from her. She was still in a heavy sleep. His head turned, looking up at each corner of the ceiling where Aiden had installed tiny cameras that you could barely see with the naked eye. It gave a full view of the bed and entire room.

He tightened the silk robe he was wearing as he approached the edge of the bed. His eyes trailed her long legs up to the juncture between her thighs. His gaze rested on her pussy that was covered with pink sheer lace panties.

Fuck, she was beautiful, he thought. He continued his gaze up her flat stomach to the small tee shirt she was wearing. Her nipples had hardened beneath the thin fabric from the coldness in the air. Her full lips, creamy olive skin, and dark sooty lashes were making his cock stir below in his robe. Not wanting to wait for a second longer, he moved quickly and placed the pliable rubber bracelets to her wrists and ankles and reached out, brushing his thumbs over her taut nipples. He cupped one full breast in his palm, squeezing slightly and then rubbed the stiff peak. His eyes ran to her face when she moaned softly in her sleep at his touch.

Losing his control, he squeezed tightly around the one breast and she licked her lips and moaned again. He leaned over and slid his hand along her inner thigh, his thumb and fingers lightly grazing her pussy through

the fabric.

"Mmm..." She moved slightly. Lucas could feel his excitement build as the blood flowed down to his cock at the sight before him and the events that were about to play out. He slid his hands along her arms and grasped her

wrists, his face only an inch from hers as he whispered.

JESSA JAMES

"Reagan, wake up." His fingers once again grazed her pussy lips over the fabric and she stirred. "Wake up Reagan." He whispered again.

He watched as she slowly opened her eyes trying to adjust to the darkness. Her eyes fluttered open and then they focused on him. Her eyes were wide orbs of hazel and instantly filled with fear and confusion.

"What the fu-" She said.

~

*R*eagan was in utter shock. When her brain finally comprehended what the fuck was happening she totally lost it. Ferris was covered in only a silk robe and when she tried to sit up, she discovered she was bound to the bed. Panic consumed her as she realized the bastard had tied her up! She strained uselessly against the bonds and screamed. "AIDEN! HELP! Please help me, Aiden!"

Ferris clamped a hand over her mouth, silencing her. "Shhh," he growled. "No one is going to save you, Reagan." She stared up at him and all she saw was malevolent gems. There was no compassion in his dark blue eyes. No guilt or sympathy. Reagan didn't believe him as she glared at him, waiting for her brother to respond to her scream. There was only silence. No one came as the minutes passed by, the two of them with their eyes locked on one another.

"Reagan, there is no need to scream." He removed his hand slowly from her mouth and smiled.

"What the fuck are you doing? Why am I tied up?" she spat.

Unbelievably he lowered his head and nuzzled her neck, answering, "You're part of this weekend's business deal, I'm afraid." He licked and nipped her earlobe sharply with his teeth, making her gasp and fight the restraints once again. "Aiden made this deal so appealing, that I just couldn't refuse."

Lucas shifted his weight and laid his hands back on her breasts, kneading them through her tee shirt.

"Take your fucking hands off me!" She narrowed her eyes at him, willing every bit of angry hatred she felt in her words. "Conducting a business deal with my brother doesn't entitle you to feel me up!"

A devilish grin pulled at his lips. "Oh but you're wrong Reagan. You are the biggest part of the business deal. Fuck, you taste so good," He growled, his breath hot against her neck. "Like vanilla."

Reagan strained and twisted her body in an effort to get the bastard off of her but it was useless. It only made him laugh. "You're insane. My brother would never do this."

Ferris raised his head, staring down at her and cocked an eyebrow. "Are you sure about that? I'm taking over your brother's business, Reagan and you were part of that deal whether you like it or not."

"You're fucking crazy!" She spat through gritted teeth. He rolled her nipples rough between his fingers as he let out a deep laugh. "You don't know your step-brother very well. I assure you he has and in the fine print of the addendum he signed tonight, he gave you to me."

"Fuck you! You're lying. AIDEN!" She screamed. "What did you do to him?"

Ferris let out another amused laugh and then stood up, shaking his head, and opened the bedroom door. When she turned her head and saw her brother standing there, she froze. It felt as though all the blood in her body had just been drained. Her brain refused to function or try to adapt to the reality of what was happening. This can't be happening. No! He was the only family she had left. How could he do this?

"Aiden?" Confusion marred Reagan's features.

"Do what he says, Reagan," her brother said coldly without emotion. It was like an icy dagger had just impaled her heart.

"Aiden? No! You can't do this! Please, you can't be serious?" She felt the first tear roll down the side of her cheek as she looked at her brother's vacant icy stare. "You're the only family I have Aiden. Please don't do this to me. Please." She begged.

Lucas shook his head and firmly ushered her brother back into the hallway. She could hear them talking in whispered tones and couldn't make out what they were saying. This has to be a fucking nightmare. How could he do this to her? She loved him, was always loyal to him. Fuck!

CHAPTER 3

Shutting the door behind him, Lucas came back in the room. The dark predator bore down on her, a wicked hunger in his dark blue eyes.

"Your brother negotiated an extra million out of me by ensuring you're a virgin. That was a surprise bonus, and I was content to pay the extra money."

His eyes swept over her body, making her feel hot from head to toe and fear gripped her not knowing what he was going to do to her.

"If you knew me, Reagan, you'd know that there are two things at which I excel. Two very important things that drive me. Business and sex. This deal allows me to satisfy both cravings at once." He said with a devilish grin.

Ferris climbed onto the bed next to her, laying his hand on her stomach, lightly tracing circles around her belly button. "I'm not going to hurt you, but I will most definitely have you, Reagan. Whether you like it or not. Nothing you say will stop me. Nothing you do will change the fact that I'm going to fuck you. Very soon...and very hard."

Her mouth wouldn't work. She tried and she could feel her heartbeat speed up and pound through her chest. She could only watch in silence as he slipped his hand under the elastic of her panties and pushed a long thick finger through the little airstrip of pubic hair she had. When his finger reached the moistness that had begun to gather between her pussy lips, she shuddered as pleasure saturated her body, despite her rejection and the fact she was scared to death.

His blue eyes flashed wickedly and a grin pulled at the corners of his full lips as he felt her wetness. "So wet, this will make it much easier on you."

Lucas pulled up her shirt exposing her taut nipples. He bent down and took one nipple in his hot, wet mouth. As he sucked on it, his finger continued to probe her pussy, massaging her own creamy arousal into her skin. He pushed his finger further inside to verify her virginity, satisfied when

he felt a barrier to his intrusion. Reagan's breath hitched when she realized that she was enjoying his touch. It made her feel dirty and she thrashed and bucked against him, taking him by surprise.

"Get off me you sick fuck!" She screamed. "You can't do this!"

His smile turned into an evil grin. "Oh but I can Reagan, and I will."

"When this is done, you'll be spending the rest of your sorry ass in jail. You must be pretty desperate to have to purchase women to get fucked."

Just then her eyes widened like saucers and she gasped when she watched him straddle her body. He grabbed some pillows and shoved them behind her to prop her head up. In the process, his robe opened up slightly allowing her to get a glimpse at his rock hard cock. This close to her face, it seemed already impossibly large.

"This will shut you up!" He growled inching his way up to her face.

She watched in horror as he got closer. "You mean gag me?" she faltered, eyes wide.

He grinned and removed his belt, tossing it aside. "Oh no. Not with my belt." He growled as his eyes imprisoned hers and then moved up until his cock was inches from her face. Her heart skipped a beat at his words. His eyes were rivers of fervor, dragging her under, threatening to choke her. She quickly sucked in a breath and let it out as if she were about to start hyperventilating.

"Please don't." She cried feeling the tears fall down the sides of her cheeks. "You can't! I've never done this before." She said her fear turning to anger. Reagan strained uselessly against her bonds.

"There's a first time for everything," he assured her. "I'm sure I won't be disappointed." Lucas took his hard cock in his hand and thumbed the head as he pressed it to her tightly closed lips. Stroking her lips with the silken head, back and forth, a creamy drop of pre-cum oozed out. He smoothed it over her tightly clamped lips, while she stared up at him in horror and then defiance blazed in her eyes.

"Open for me, Reagan. Open your mouth now!"

She narrowed her eyes and quickly shook her head. Out of impatience, he took a handful of hair with the other hand and shook her head roughly. "Open!" he bellowed.

Terrified by the violence in his voice and the sharp pain in her scalp, she opened her mouth. The moment she did, he pushed inside, engorged and pulsating. With a deep breath, Lucas recovered his control. He stroked slowly in and out an inch or so, to get her accustomed to the hard hot cock in her mouth. When she looked up at him, her eyes were wide with fear, so he spoke softly to her.

"That's a good girl. Just like that," he groaned. "Lick it, use your tongue..."

Reagan couldn't. All she could do was look up at him, in a complete daze because the man above her was fucking her mouth and there wasn't a damn thing she could do about it.

Lucas braced himself on the headboard with his hands and started to rock his hips back and forth, slowly going deeper and deeper with each stroke. She heard his long and controlled breaths and the wet sounds his cock made when it slid in and out of her mouth. And, oh, fucking God, she heard a tiny whimpering sound that erupted from her own throat.

"Relax, honey," he whispered. "I'm going to go deeper. Jesus, so fucking incredible!"

Reagan clenched her hands into fists as she felt him push his thick hard cock to the back of her throat, gagging her just as he promised. His eyes fluttered shut and she could see a sheen layer of sweat on his face.

"Christ!"

Lucas sucked in a ragged breath through gritted teeth. He just kept picturing that wide-eyed look of fear on her face when she realized he was going to push his cock into her mouth. That image, along with the feeling of her innocent lips wrapped around his hard cock drove him closer to his climax. On the seventh stroke, he couldn't help himself and gave a hoarse grunt when he erupted into her mouth. He gripped the headboard as profound pleasure ripped through him from his cock and balls washing over his entire body. When he finally looked down at her, he saw his cum leaking out of the corners of her mouth, and his flat abdomen wore spatters of it.

"Oh, Reagan. That was very good. Very, very good. I'm going to pull out now, but I want your mouth open." As he withdrew his cock from between her glistening lips he watched her with narrowed eyes, to see if she would obey. Lifting her chin in dissent, she spat his cum at him, spraying his stomach with it. Reagan's eyes burned with defiance.

Lucas closed his eyes and he shook his head. He admired her spirit; however, he didn't show it. "Open your mouth," he repeated.

Looking up at him, she only stared. He found her nipple and twisted harshly until she cried out and then finally obeyed, glaring up at him. With his hand, he milked more cum out of his cock and let it dribble onto her tongue.

"Swallow!" He watched Reagan's throat closely as she hesitantly complied. He rose to his knees and let out some slack in her restraints. Turning away, Reagan wiped her face on the pillowcase as he stretched out on his side next to her. His cock, still heavy with blood, laid on his thigh.

"Come and lick me clean. I've loosened your bonds." He gestured at his stomach, spotted with his white cum. "Don't rebel, Reagan. You don't want to find out what happens if you do."

Her eyes were full of disgust as she bent over him and lapped at the droplets on his skin. He watched her pink tongue dart out to take up the thick splatters of cum and felt himself growing hard once again.

Reagan shuddered with a mixture of revulsion and excitement as Lucas leaned forward and grasped the back of her neck. He pulled her up to him and kissed her, pushing his tongue past the seam of her lips to seek entry. She could still taste the lingering pungency of his cum.

A smile erupted across his face as he rose off the bed, and grabbed his satchel, disappearing into the bathroom that was adjoined to the bedroom.

CHAPTER 4

While he was gone, Reagan took the opportunity to try and free herself. There was enough slack now that she could examine the bracelets closely. She tried to flick the switch back and forth but it only accomplished loosening and then tightening the one side. Damn it!

Lucas' low laugh from the bathroom startled her. She watched him return from the bathroom and then stop. He held up his hand, wagging his finger at her back and forth. "Tsk, tsk. That won't work. But this will." He grinned holding up a little key. "You're mine until I'm done."

He took a few steps towards the bed while holding something in his hand. After setting the object down, he adjusted her wrist restraints so her arms were again outstretched and then removed her ankle bracelets completely. She immediately clamped her legs together tightly, causing a frown to

mar his features. "Spread your legs," he ordered in a soft voice, but it was clearly a command, not a request. She watched as he grabbed the object he had laid down. Panic seized her as he climbed onto the bed and removed her lace panties, exposing her virgin pussy.

"Mmm." He groaned as his fingers spread her velvety lips. "Bare as a baby's bum." Reagan had always hated pubic hair so she only kept a little strip on top. As his fingers played with her pussy, her legs began to close once again. He looked up at her as he pushed her legs apart. "Wider, Reagan."

She closed her eyes, finally giving in and allowing both of her legs to fall to either side giving him full access. She was frightened, yet excited at the same time not knowing what would happen next. At the buzzing sound, she opened her eyes. He slowly slid the small bullet up and down her soft wet folds and secret crevices, igniting every nerve in her pussy. She didn't even breathe, exhaling only when he pulled away. Sometimes he would use his fingers to pull her pussy lips apart and slowly penetrate just the tip of the vibrator in her entrance. In and out, in and out. She could feel the erotic pulsing between her legs.

"You're so fucking wet, Reagan," he observed with a crooked smile and his eyes flashed wickedly. She could feel her face burn with shame as her body defied her. Lucas had aroused her more than she'd ever been aroused before, and his dominance and control only added to it.

He nudged her thigh impatiently. "Wider." She opened her legs even more. This time she felt the little bullet enter her ass. Just the outside of the ring and every time it inched a little further a naughty thrill would race through her. Reagan couldn't understand why her body was acting like this. Jesus Christ! What the hell was wrong with her that a man who was forcing her to be his sexual plaything was turning her on? Had she completely lost it?

Lucas turned the vibrator speed up a notch and started pumping her pussy only at the entrance. She couldn't help the moan that escaped her lips as the sensation built. "Mmm. You like that don't you?" He asked continuing to drive her over the edge. He pulled the vibrator out and turned it off, laying it on the bed. Her bare pussy, all silk, and pouty pink flesh glistened with her juices.

He was suddenly overwhelmed with a deep hunger for her innocent sweetness; the need to feel her satiny pussy lips with his tongue consumed him. More than anything he craved to feel her buck against his face as he licked her, teased her and sucked the intoxicating juices directly from her virgin cunt.

A deep low gruntal sound came from deep in his throat as he lunged forward and buried his face between her thighs. Reagan flinched in surprise. His hands gripped her knees, pushing them open, forcing her legs to spread. His tongue, hot and slick, licked at her, delving between the folds of her lips, edging around her sensitive clit. Reagan felt him circle her swollen entrance with his lips. She had never let anyone get this close to her pussy and was dismayed at the intense pleasure taking over her body as he feasted on her like a hungry animal. She felt her control slipping away as her hips moved of their own violation toward his glorious mouth. With each pull, lick and suck, she felt the heat consume her which only increased the desperation of her need for a release. Reagan had pleasured herself thousands of times, but she had never felt this type of intensity before.

She was going mad with pleasure and all she wanted to do was grind her pussy against his face in a wordless demand to bring her to climax. At that moment, only his lips and tongue were her world. She tried to hold back the gruntal sounds and moans but it was useless. Her body was betraying her, and she had no control anymore and at that point, she didn't care. She needed release, she needed to cum. Oh, Jesus Christ, she was going to cum!

Lucas knew Reagan was about to lose all control and give in to the orgasm; he had been watching her intently, each and every thrust of her hips and the louder her moans became. Every time her pussy pulsed against his chin, his thick cock throbbed in response. He thrilled to every strangled whimper that escaped her lips. Fuck it was erotic! When he watched her finally reach the peak of excitement, he stopped, leaving her to falter on the edge of a violent, orgasm. She twisted against her restraints in frustration, panting heavily, but he only smirked at her, his face covered in her juices.

"Screw you, you sick fuck!" she cried out and shut her eyes trying to regain her breathing.

"You want me so fucking bad, don't you Reagan?" He said

looking at her clit, that was beautifully swollen from the onslaught of his mouth. He touched a fingertip to her pouty opening and laughed when her pussy convulsed in an attempt to pull his finger in.

"Stop. Please." She sounded defeated. "You're making me do this!"

Lucas smiled. Despite the fact that her cunt was dripping, she was denying her own obvious pleasure. He had to admit, she was stubborn but he was up to the challenge. He teased her even more by drawing his finger around the outer edges of those baby-soft lips, amused by the pulsating spasms it caused.

"Reagan, honey. You're going to beg me to fuck you." He placed a hand behind her knee, raising one of her legs up, and rubbed her clit with the fleshy pad of his finger.

"Fuck!" Reagan panted, her body tense and unmoving except for the twitches that came from her soaking pussy.

He moved up the bed until his knees hugged her flanks. He bent his head down and said, "You'll be begging me to take your virginity."

"Fuck you!" she spat gasping for a breath, the sweat trickling down her temples into her long strawberry blonde hair. She bit her lip and turned away.

"Come on, beg me to fuck you senseless..."

"No!" she retorted firmly as he slid his cock against her sensitive clit teasing her.

"...mmm...to give you that release you so desperately want." As he stroked her slowly with his hard cock, he sucked in a breath, fighting his own urge to cum.

With impatience, he lifted her other leg up and concentrated on driving her to desperation instead. "Feels good, doesn't it, Reagan," he growled, "my thick cock sliding against your swollen wet folds."

She let out a whimper when he pushed his hips in a rapid series of thrusts. The friction against her pussy was driving her mad.

"Think of the pleasure you'll feel, having my cock inside you, filling you. It would feel so fucking good. All you have to do is say the word, Reagan. Just tell me you want it."

Her hands were clenched into fists as her breath came in quick pants and she stubbornly said nothing. She wasn't going to give him the satisfaction.

Lucas grinned. He could play this game and he was happy to oblige. He released her leg and moved over her straining body. With a smooth pivot of his hips, he pushed just the head of his pulsing cock into her. Balancing his weight on his arms, the only part of his body that touched her was his cock.

Her body jerked and her gaze flew to his. "No, please don't!"

He watched the fear in her eyes and it excited him but then he had an irrational urge to comfort her. "That's only the head, Reagan," he whispered. "Just relax. It's going to feel so good. I promise." She sucked in a deep breath and closed her eyes. He felt her body relax silently. "That's a good girl." His words came out softly as he rocked his hips and entered her again and again, letting only the head slip inside and then out again. Her cunt was so tight that the tip of his cock made a loud sucking sound as it went in and out. He watched her face carefully, gauging her reaction, and her body's response as he altered his speed, sometimes pulling out and sliding the length of the head against her twitching, swollen clit, only to slip inside again. That bare inch teasing her a little more. Within moments he felt the unconscious shifting of her hips matching the rhythm of his movements. The response spoke volumes.

She was letting go of her inhibitions, going beyond her fears and allowing the pleasure to take over, allowing herself to get lost in it.

"That's it sweet thing. It feels so good, doesn't it? Tell me you want it. Beg me, Reagan." He leaned down whispering in her ear, "Tell me you want to feel my cock inside you."

Reagan kept her mouth shut and her eyes closed.

"Fuck, you feel so good. You want it deep inside you, don't

you, Reagan? All this teasing is driving you crazy." He moved his hips quickly, allowing just the head of his cock to slip in and out, making her pant and thrash. "The only way for release is to say it, Reagan. Tell me you want it and I'll let you cum. Beg me to fuck you!"

As she edged closer and closer to a climax, he pushed her more urgently. Tiny beads of perspiration formed on her forehead and she started moaning and panting a little more harshly but tried to keep it under control. Lucas was sweating himself from the effort it took to withhold his own orgasm. When she had built up to her climax again, he again denied her. With a quick jerk of his hips, he withdrew, leaving her swollen pussy aching and empty.

"No, please! Please!" She arched off the bed toward him almost involuntarily. He ignored her but kept her primed with soothing strokes of his fingers on her swollen clit.

"Please what, Reagan?" He squeezed the head of his cock tightly to postpone his own release. The buttery feel of her pussy lips against and around the tip of his cock was utter torture and his cock pulsed in his hand, but he didn't climax.

"Fuck!" she gasped, struggling with her pride. She hated needing something from him, but she needed release like she needed her last breath. Her pussy ached and throbbed with a harsh need that she had never felt before and she finally let go, not giving a fuck anymore.

"Fuck me, you sick bastard!" She cried.

Lucas stared into her hazel eyes and shook his head. "You can do much better than that."

Reagan bit her lip as he shifted down and licked her between her legs again. The feeling of his hot tongue on her sent a shiver through her body and every nerve was focused on her engorged clit. Again, he brought her back to the edge and let her hang there. Once it subsided, he did it again and again until she couldn't think anymore and she was a quivering mess.

"Please, I'm begging you. Please, fuck me. Fuck me!"

He gave her one last long suck of her aching clit with his mouth and made her jump. "More." He growled as he sucked one of her pussy lips gently and pushed two fingers into her juicy cunt. She couldn't stop her body from bucking up against him.

"PLEASE! I beg you. Fuck me. Shove it in. Please!" She cried out.

*L*ucas slid up her body, stopping to suck hard on a nipple and she gasped at the sensation. Her body was on fire.

With a savage smile of victory, Lucas positioned himself above her, lined his cock at her entrance and pushed. She was so smooth that if she hadn't been a virgin, he might have slipped right in. She was so very, very tight which excited him because he intended to make it excruciatingly slow, so he could feel the tear of her virginity under the onslaught of his hard thick cock.

"Oh God," she whimpered.

As soon as he slowly pushed inside her, Reagan wasn't sure she wanted this after all. The throbbing thickness just kept coming, deeper and deeper until he butted up against the supple, virginal barrier-not hard enough to rip it, but enough to test its resilience. She felt like he would rip her in two. Reagan writhed under his body, trying to move away from the steady, painful pressure of his invasion. She'd never had anything in there thicker than her finger.

"N-n-n-no...," she cried. "It hurts-" She panted as he pushed again. Lucas stopped, breathing hard. "Jesus Christ, you're fucking tight." He brushed away a strand of hair from her face and whispered. "You need to relax and it won't hurt so much."

Lucas reached down and strummed her clit with his fingers bringing her back up again towards that fantastic orgasm. Heavy pants started to come from her throat. Using just the right amount of pressure he stroked her clit with such intensity and this time let the orgasm take hold. Reagan cried out and strained against her bonds as the erotic orgasm ripped through her body. Her vice-like cunt convulsed around him, squeezing him mercilessly. She even cried out his name while she was in the midst of her orgasmic spasms.

He bore down on her again with a relentless pressure, this time not stopping when he felt the vigilant resistant of her virginity; he reveled in the pleasure of breaking her sweet barrier, pushing deeper and deeper. He was obsessed with an inescapable need to be buried deep inside of her.

"Oh fuck yes," he growled. At last, his balls nestled against her anus as he ground himself against her with a rumbling moan of pleasure. Lucas began to move slow and deliver deep rhythmic and penetrating strokes even though she was still incredibly tight. He knew the longer he forced himself to wait, the more intense his orgasm would be. He looked down at Reagan and the more he moved the more her face relaxed, though she still seemed to be fighting the building pleasure. When her legs wrapped his hips and she rocked upward against him, he knew she was beyond the pain and it drove him over the edge.

"It feels good, doesn't it Reagan? Eight inches of hard cock inside your cunt. Can you feel every inch of it fill you up as I push into you?" He increased his tempo of strokes and the friction of their fucking was almost electric and when she let out a gasping cry, he pounded her hard.

"Oh fuck yes, cum for me, little one." He groaned and thrust into her harder, his hips pumping like a well-oiled machine. From the corner of his eye, he could see her fist opening and closing within her restraints, but her panting cries were encouraging him to continue.

"Jesus Christ!" he grunted into her neck. "I'm going to cum inside you, Reagan." At his words, her body went rigid for a moment. Then she bucked up against him, collapsing into wracking shudders as her second orgasm consumed her entire body. When her cunt clenched him in tight, undulate, repetitive grips, his head dropped forward and he came. With a guttural cry, he exploded inside her. His cock convulsed as his load erupted from him in prolonged spurts. Every muscle in his body tensed as he pulled out. Looking down at his cock in his hand he could see Reagan's glistening virginal blood on it. The sight of the crimson stain on his skin filled him with satisfaction.

"Christ, Reagan, you're a great fuck." He bent down and kissed her deeply and then gave her breast a squeeze. "And it's only going to get better the next time."

Reagan fought her tears of shame as she realized that he wasn't going to be satisfied with only taking her virginity. Lucas had an agenda and she had no idea what it was. She did know that her ordeal was far from over.

CHAPTER 5

*L*ucas thought if only every business deal could end up with him fucking a gorgeous virgin. He sat back, utterly amused at the sight of Reagan pretending she was sleeping. Her long blond hair was in a glorious array on the pillows, her stomach dotted with his sperm. Between the juncture of her thighs, he saw more of his cum mixed with her virginal blood, seeping out of her glistening pussy. He couldn't resist and dipped a finger into her sticky warmth, coated it, and then wiped it on her lips. Reagan jerked and opened her eyes, betraying the fact that she wasn't sleeping.

His eyes were trained on hers when he said, "I'm going to release you, Reagan."

A wave of excitement filled her. Maybe she had been wrong and it was over after all and she could try and forget this hateful assault had ever happened — try to convince herself that she hadn't enjoyed it.

In one fluid motion, Lucas rose from the bed exposing the dips and planes of his athletic body. Despite the fact that this man had just force-fucked her, she had to admire the perfection of his body. He had to have worked out every day to develop a physique like that she thought. Each muscle in his body was beautifully defined. Her eyes were suddenly drawn to his cock, streaked with a mixture of cum and her blood. She remembered how full she felt and the violent orgasm that rocked her body in oblivion and her pussy twitched as if it yearned for more. Jesus, Reagan! It was purely her body reacting, her body's reflex to stimulation.

Lucas chuckled and snapped his fingers bringing her gaze to his face. He looked amused as if he knew what she had been thinking. "I'm going to let you wash up." He said, as he leaned over her, and unlocked her restraints around her wrists. Reagan sat up and rubbed her wrists. "Take as long as you like but only take a shower, not a bath."

She walked to the bathroom and noticed the knob was missing and turned back to look at him. Lucas shrugged his shoulders and gave her a gesture with his hand to enter. She turned on the water for the shower and stepped in.

∽

Lucas walked to the intercom on the wall and pressed the button. "I hope you're there Aiden."

"I'm here."

"Did you watch? Listen?"

"Oh God, yes," Aiden sounded excited.

"I hope you enjoyed it as much as I did." Lucas grinned to himself.

"Fuck you, Lucas. I want my piece." He growled into the intercom.

"Once we finalize the deal and sign on the dotted line, you can have any piece of her you like. The night is still young and there is much more play to do. Oh and bring me up a bottle of bourbon with two glasses." Lucas pushed another button, locking the intercom on transmission only.

Before Aiden and Reagan's parents died in the car accident, Lucas' father, Rex had acquired over twenty different land deals with Sean Lynch, Aiden's father, and Reagan's step-father. When Aiden took over the business Rex and Lucas watched as he slowly drove it into the ground and thought what a fucking disgrace it was. How disappointed his father would have been if he were still alive. When Lucas came along and initiated a takeover bid, he knew that Aiden would sell what was left of the company without a blink of an eye. He had been screwing things up for the last year and it showed in the earnings reports. When Lucas Ferris made the offer, his father, Rex, ordered his team to propose a half-hearted counteroffer. And so it began.

Lucas dragged out the negotiations on purpose, carefully calculating the right moment to see if Aiden would jump on his request. At one meeting, Reagan had slipped into the room, making every single man straighten up in his seat. She wore a white sheer, billowing blouse unbuttoned to the waist which revealed the tight tank top and a short skort skirt. Lucas had carefully been watching Aiden for a very long time when it came to his behavior with his step-sister.

"Reagan, what a nice surprise," Aiden would say and smile. Lucas wasn't surprised. He had arranged her entrance and it wasn't uncommon for him to use his step-sister's striking beauty to distract his business adversaries. He nodded with approval when he noticed her nipples were erect. She would stop short as if she hadn't known that the room would be full of people.

"I'm so sorry. I thought you would be ready to leave by now, Aiden. I didn't mean to interrupt."

Lucas stood, enjoying the view before him. "Not at all, Reagan. I think everyone here would agree that this type of interruption is quite welcomed." Reagan smiled as Aiden made the introductions. Aiden also noticed Lucas' interest in Reagan and agreed to have dinner with them that night.

The following day, Lucas had insisted on a private meeting at their family estate in La Jolla, California. When Lucas arrived, he didn't waste any time and handed Aiden a thick file. "Take your time reading it over. I'll have a drink in the meantime." Lucas said, pouring the amber liquid into a glass.

Aiden had read the documents twice and looked over at Lucas. A wicked smile pulling at the corners of his lips. "You fucker!" He said, walking over to Lucas and then slapped him on the back. "I'll do it, but change it to a few hours and I get second dibs."

Lucas drained the last of his drink and laid the glass down and reached out for the file. "You sick fuck. Deal's off." He tucked the file under his arm and headed for the door.

"Oh come on now, Lucas. Jesus Christ. She's my step-sister, not blood."

He turned and stared at the piece of shit. "I'll give you one more chance. Don't be fucking stupid. I want her for twenty-four hours to use as I wish. Not an hour less or an hour more. In exchange, I will defer to every single original item that you listed during the initial negotiations, and pay the full purchase price."

Aiden didn't hesitate as the smile crept across his face. "She's a virgin, you know," Aiden said shrewdly. "Five million for her cherry."

Lucas stood still, not even blinking an eyelash. "Insane."

"Ok, two million then. I guarantee she'll be worth it."

"Two hundred and fifty thousand," Lucas replied.

A frown marred Aiden's features. "Did I mention her tits are like-"

Aiden stopped talking as Reagan passed by wearing the most scandalous bathing suit. Aiden couldn't contain his smile. Perfect timing, he thought.

Both watched as she smiled at them and walked out back to the pool. When she was gone, Aiden chuckled and said, "Three, no lower."

"One. Final offer."

With a couple of minor conditions, they verbally sealed the deal which would be signed the following month and Lucas left their estate with a smile on his face. If Aiden only knew what had just happened his head would spin.

~

When Aiden delivered the bourbon and glasses to his sister's bedroom, Lucas ordered him to return to his room and then closed the door on him. Sick voyeuristic bastard, Lucas thought to himself. He set the bottle and glasses on the side table and grabbed his satchel and retrieved a few candles. He lit them, giving the space a light orange glow. Bright light spilled from the bathroom where Reagan was still in the shower. He was sure she was washing away off all of the cum from her body and he decided to check on her.

The oversized luxurious shower had twin nozzles and a built in marble bench. Through the steamy glass doors, Lucas could see the blurred outline of Reagan. He could see her hands pressed against the wall while the water showered down onto her long locks. He could see the tantalizing view of her back and her delicious round ass. His cock twitched and he licked his lips as he thought about licking between those ass cheeks, feeling the puckered hole of her anus with his tongue.

Time for round two.

He took a second to press the button on the intercom which activated voice and the cameras. He watched her intently, his eyes feasting on her lush body. He grabbed his hardening cock and started to stroke it. Lucas watched as she reached for the soap, not noticing him yet and worked up a lather, caressing her own breasts. Fuck, she had great tits! He couldn't wait to suck on them again, feel them in his large hands and roll those hard nipples between his thumb and forefinger. His mouth went dry when she reached down to wash her pussy. Her fingers delving between her legs and around and between the twin globes of her firm young ass finally drove him to pounce his prey once again.

In one fluid motion, he slid the shower door open and entered the hot steamy enclosure. Reagan quickly turned around with a gasp. Her eyes flew down to the sight of his raging hard on, thrusting outward like a steel pole and she backed up against the tile wall.

"I thought you said I could take a shower?" she hissed clenching her fists.

"Turn around." Lucas gave her a predatory grin. She did as she was told, not wanting to fight him. The hot droplets cascaded down on them both and the heat felt amazing. How convenient that she had a shower big enough for a few people. He placed his hands on her hips rubbing her soapy skin as the head of his stiff cock poked her ass cheeks.

His lips nestled by her ear and he whispered, "Let's fuck, Reagan." He knew Aiden would be listening and watching. He was a sick fuck in Lucas' eyes. "Let's have some fun and change the game up. You tell me how you want it this time." His hand slid up her torso until he reached her full breasts. He squeezed them and felt her nipples harden under his touch. He rolled them between his fingers and bent over and nipped at her neck gently. Reagan began to pant and felt her hips move against him.

"Tell me exactly how you want me to fuck you." He continued to tweak one nipple as his other hand slid down and found her clit. While he stroked her sensitive nub and tweaked her nipple, he had her squirming with pleasure in a matter of minutes. "I was going to fuck that pretty little ass of yours," he said in a deep, husky voice. Her cunt clamped around his finger just as he finished his sentence.

"What?" He laughed. "You like that idea, don't you?"

She only turned her face away. He took his finger from her wet pussy and circled the pinched hole of her virgin ass.

"Mmm." he groaned.

She shuddered in his arms and a low moan rippled from her throat. Smiling to himself, he slicked up his finger and pushed it into her asshole. Reagan moaned louder. Keeping his finger in her ass, he reached around with his other hand and plunged two fingers into her cunt.

"Fuck, you're so wet, Reagan," he murmured into her ear. "Oh, you like it when I play with your ass."

"No," she cried weakly. "Stop, don't make me..."

Lucas pumped his fingers in and out of her asshole and grinned, loving every second of it. "I don't have to make you do anything, little one. You're pussy is soaking wet for me, and certainly not because of the shower. Your clit is throbbing against my finger and your heart is racing. Your body is screaming to be fucked up the ass."

"Fuck you!" she hissed and turned around causing his fingers to pop out of her pussy and anus. Her eyes blazed with defiance as she held his stare not backing down. His eye's narrowed and they looked like angry swirls of dark blue. As she stood under the pelting stream of water, she knew she made a mistake.

Lucas pinned her with a rigid stare that sent a shiver down her body and then took her by the arms, pinning them up, over her head against the tile. "I don't think you understand. I'm in charge here. You are here for MY enjoyment. I bought you." He paused holding her arms in a steely grip. "You fucking loved what I did to you earlier. Fucking loved it! Though you were too afraid to admit it."

Reagan gaped at him in shock. "Yes, Reagan. You begged me to fuck you. The sooner you admit it, the sooner you'll accept it."

She shook her head again. "Stop saying that. I had no choice."

His face was only an inch away from hers. "You came, Reagan. Twice and you fucking loved it!" He snarled.

She looked at him with vengeance in her eyes. "You sadistic son of a bitch!"

He laughed. "You don't have a fucking clue what sadistic is, Reagan. But you're about to find out."

CHAPTER 6

He forced her down on her knees, fisted a hand in her strawberry blonde hair and pulled back so that her chin tilted up and he could clearly see her large doe shaped hazel eyes. His cock jutted out in front of her.

"Suck my cock." He growled.

He braced himself so that one hand was against the tile wall and his feet were against the bench. This allowed him to angle his body for more extreme penetration if this is what he chose.

A devilish grin pulled to his lips as he watched her open her mouth and he shoved his cock inside. He plunged deeply and concentrated on his cock disappearing into her beautiful mouth. His balls slapped against her chin as he rocked his hips and rammed himself down her throat. Fuck! Only a few minutes passed and with complete torture, he pulled out groaning.

"Up." He commanded. Lucas watched her obey. "Turn around."

He grasped her hip and pushed her shoulder to bend her forward. Then he kicked her feet apart with his own to spread her legs. Absolutely perfect. Bending his knees, he angled the head of his hard cock at her entrance and shoved. This was not the careful, indulgent coupling he'd given her earlier. He didn't give a shit whether she came or not or gave any attention to her pleasure. All he wanted was to exert his power over her. This was pure animalistic fury. He pounded her so hard that her feet kept sliding. Every hard thrust, he gave a loud grunt, only because it felt so fucking good and he knew her brother was listening.

"You're so...uuh!...fucking...uuh!...tight," he growled out the words between grunts. He felt the jerk of his cock as he shot his cum deep inside her as the water cascaded down on both of them.

When he caught his breath, he pulled out and Reagan backed up against the wall. Ignoring her, he grabbed the soap and washed himself off. He rinsed, took one last glance at her and then left the shower, grabbing a towel before leaving the bathroom. This was crazy; he would not feel bad about what he had just done.

A few moments later he heard the water stop running. She wrapped herself in a towel and then dried her hair with a smaller towel. As she walked out of the bathroom, he guided her to the bed.

His eyes locked with hers. "No restraints for now." He said gesturing her to get under the covers and then poured her a glass of bourbon. "Drink this. Then we should get some sleep."

Reagan drank the liquor in one shot. She wasn't a fan, but right now she needed it. She closed her eyes and shook her head as the liquor left a fiery trail down her throat and warmed her belly. She was utterly exhausted and could barely move. Her arms and legs felt like jelly as she lay down. The clock read four twenty-five. No wonder she was so tired.

Lucas climbed into bed next to her and finished his glass of bourbon. Her rhythmic breathing and her lovely face made him feel strangely sated, almost a feeling of content. Normally every waking moment was about business. Always extending his reach in his corporate deals. Even during sex, he would be thinking about business and the next approach on how to increase his bottom dollar. His sexual satisfaction was the only thing that equaled his drive for wealth and power. But since he had first met Reagan, everything seemed nonexistent to him. Reagan did something to him, that he couldn't even understand himself. His vast corporate empire continued without him, as it should. Lucas hired only the most competent executives that could run his business for several weeks without him, but for once he was free from the burden of his business and could solely focus on the situation that was playing out now.

After blowing out the candle, he closed his eyes as he lay next to Reagan. He needed a good night's sleep to deal with what would happen tomorrow. By mid-morning, his energy would be restored and he would be able to handle Aiden. He smiled to himself as he imagined the shocked gaping look on his face when he found out what was about to play out.

CHAPTER 7

*R*eagan stirred and slowly opened her eyes as the morning sun poured in through the window. She sat up and was pleasantly surprised to see that someone had brought up a tray that was laden with scrambled eggs, bacon, toast, and fresh fruit. There was also coffee and orange juice. For a second it felt like every other day. Not the twisted nightmare that came rushing back and consumed her thoughts.

A deep ache tore through her chest as she thought about her stepbrother. How could he do this to her? Of course, they weren't blood, but Jesus Christ, she had lived with him for nine years, as his sister! She had to have meant something to him? Their parents would be completely disgusted to learn what he had done. Even though she had played along for the last year, agreeing to his ridiculous demands, she wasn't ignorant. Reagan was well aware that her step-father had left the family business to both of them to run. Not just Aiden. She was also aware of his ignorant corporate decisions that slowly brought the family business to its knees. But she just played along, not letting on like a good little girl. She ran a hand through her long blonde hair as the anger inside of her slowly built. She was tired of playing this game. He had to fucking pay. And oh god, how she was going to make her stepbrother pay.

But for now, she would continue to play along.

The clearing of his throat caught her attention and her gaze lifted to the armchair that was in the corner of her room. Lucas sat near the window, his fingers steepled under his chin, looking at her with an intense gaze. Something inside of her stirred.

"You're awake," Lucas said grabbing his coffee cup and taking a small sip. "Eat, you'll need your energy little one."

She opened her mouth to make a comment but then promptly shut it. She stole a quick glance at the clock sitting on her nightstand. It was going on noon. Reagan sat up and looked at the food in front of her. It didn't take long to eat most of the breakfast that had been brought up to her. She was so hungry and there was no point in refusing to eat. When she finished her orange juice, she looked at Lucas and asked, "How much longer until this nightmare is over?

He cocked an eyebrow and said, "Technically until midnight but possibly sooner." He stood, grabbing a white sheer babydoll dress that lay on the bench at the end of the bed and then he placed it on the edge of the bed, indicating her to get dressed. "No bra or panties."

His words forced her mind to wander back to the fact that her own brother had given her to Lucas as a gift. Just the thought alone was sinister and she couldn't wrap her mind around it. How could anyone do this? Treat someone like a thing? Like trash as if she were fucking cattle and that she was merely a business transaction.

Aiden had used her for so long, but she never in a million years would think he was capable of being so malicious and to his own family.

Knowing he did this to her without even blinking an eye made her want to scream and rip his pretty green eyes out, but she knew she couldn't do that. She was ripped from her thoughts when Lucas whispered softly, "He's watching. Get dressed." Reagan's eyes followed his to the corners of the ceiling. She squinted trying to focus in on the little black pencil dots that now came into focus. Reagan was already angry but now that anger turned into rage and consumed her more than she thought she was capable of and the pain stabbed at her heart when the reality of last night came flooding in once again.

That sick fuck had watched everything! Omg! Reagan clutched her chest and her hand covered her mouth as she tried to contain her tears. Then her eyes went back to Lucas who was now standing at the door.

"When you're dressed, please meet me in the library." He gave her a small sad smile and shut the door behind him.

Her hand still covered her mouth as she watched him leave the room, giving her some privacy. Probably to allow her to digest the magnitude of the secret he had just shared with her. Reagan felt a tear roll down her cheek and then sucked in a deep breath and roughly wiped the tear away with the back of her hand. Oh, she was fucking pissed.

She stood up, fully naked and walked to the edge of the bed, grabbing the dress. She was seething inside and knew she had to get a handle on herself. Aiden wanted to watch her get raped, to see her vulnerable and have her most intimate parts be exposed and ruined by a man that he had gifted her too. Well, she would fucking show him.

Reagan walked slowly to the bathroom holding the dress in her hand, taking in deep breaths to calm herself. She slipped into the small white sheer garment and then grabbed the sink with both hands, looking at herself in the mirror. She thought about the small cameras that were in her bedroom and turned around slowly, trying not to be obvious as she inspected the bathroom ceiling and walls. She saw two more cameras flanking the shower. She turned to look at herself again and grabbed her brush, slowly smoothing out her long blond hair. "You can do this, Reagan. You can do this." The words rushed through her thoughts as she brushed her hair calmly.

Walking around without panties felt strange. Every step she took brought a breath of air up under her dress. A few moments later, Reagan padded down the hallway, walked downstairs and entered the library as she was told to do so earlier. Her eyes instantly fell on her brother. Sitting in a leather chair across from a large couch where Lucas sat exchanging light conversation like it was just another fucking day. Her eyes glanced at the bodyguard who stood a few feet from the chair and then her eyes were back on Aiden.

A surge of rage threatened to swallow her as she stood there and then all eyes were on her. "Reagan. I hope you slept well?" Aiden asked with a smirk on his face.

She stood there with her arms at either side and clenched her hands into fists trying to sooth herself. She could feel her nails digging into her flesh as she plastered a smile on her face and said, "Very good."

Her eyes went to Lucas who was sitting across from her brother. "Baby doll. Come here."

Reagan slowly walked toward Lucas, never taking her eyes off of her brother. She stopped and stood beside Lucas' chair not faltering. She felt his hand slid up the back of her thigh under her dress, slowly kneading her ass cheek.

"Do you have any questions for your brother, Reagan?" He cocked an eyebrow waiting for a response and then looked at Aiden.

Reagan stole a breath before speaking, not taking her eyes off her brother. "Did you ever love me?" She whispered, watching his chin tick and then his eyes changed to something dark.

"At one point, yes. But then..." He paused trying to find the right words. "you became a commodity, something I could use as a pawn." She felt Lucas entwine his hand with hers and then give her a light squeeze as if to give her strength.

Reagan released Lucas' grip and took a step towards her brother. Through gritted teeth, she growled, "How could you? I loved you like a fucking brother you sick fuck! I was loyal!" She looked into her brother's green eyes and she saw nothing. No compassion, no guilt or even an ounce of empathy.

He held up a hand to silence her. "Enough Reagan. Spare me the drivel. I don't fucking owe you anything!" He yelled. "When I learned my father had left the family business to both of us, I was fucking furious. How dare he?! His business belonged to me, his son! Not some little fucking whore. You've been nothing but a burden and a fucking headache." Aiden looked around the room and his eyes locked with hers again. "This is merely payback, you little bitch!"

Reagan felt the tears roll down her cheeks as his words tore through her. A moment later she tucked the pain aside like she always had and let out a laugh she couldn't contain anymore. When she finally got a grip, Reagan wiped her cheeks dry and smiled. She looked over her shoulder at Lucas and asked. "Did he sign the contract, baby?"

A wicked grin appeared on Lucas' face and he nodded, "Oh, yes. He's all yours baby doll."

CHAPTER 8

Reagan turned to her brother when the words spilled from his mouth. "What the fuck?" He asked in exasperation. The perplexed look on his face made Reagan smile.

"Hmm. Who's the little bitch now, Aiden? You fucking dumbass! Doesn't feel too good does it?" She asked, standing there with each hand resting on her hips and an eyebrow cocked.

She watched as Aiden looked from her to Lucas in confusion. "Lucas, what is this? What's happening?"

"You underestimated her, Aiden. There were so many ways that you could have handled this but, unfortunately, you chose the wrong one. It's really not my concern." He returned his attention to Reagan, dismissing Aiden all together.

Reagan sat next to Lucas on the couch that sat across from her brother and curled up beside him. She ran a hand through her long hair and brought her gaze back up to the piece of shit across from her.

"You may be eleven years older than me Aiden, but you just got hustled by your nineteen-year-old sister." She smirked and grabbed the contract on the end table next to her. She held it up in the air. "This contract that you just signed gives me full control of Lynch Land Developments. It also passes all equity, stocks and family estates, including this beautiful vacation cabin." She said looking around and then her eyes landed back on her brother. Reagan held his stare, feeling completely numb inside. What love and respect she had for him amounted to nothing now. He betrayed her in the most malicious way possible and she would make sure he had nothing. Not a fucking penny. She knew this would hurt him the most. He thrived on power, status, and money. Flaunting himself as someone of importance. Now that he was penniless…not even a place to call home, she knew this would break him. She studied his face. His mouth twisted, his eyes stormy and dark as he processed what she just said.

Aiden tried to stand up in an outrage and Frankie slammed him into his seat. Reagan watched as he squeezed his hands into balled fists and gritted his teeth. "No!" He grunted as though in pain. "You can't do this to me!" He yelled. "Why would you do this? This was everything my grandfather and father built and worked so hard at. You don't deserve any of this!"

Reagan laughed. "Why? Are you fucking serious!" She closed her eyes as if to calm her annoyance and then opened them. "Aiden, this would have never happened to you. You see, it was a test and you failed miserably. This is your doing, not mine!" She seethed with rage as she spat out her words.

His features were suddenly marred with confusion again. "A test?"

Reagan sucked in a breath. "Yes, a fucking test! When it was brought to my attention months after the car accident that everything…the estates, Dad's empire and all assets were to be given to BOTH of us, I didn't believe it." She paused. "I was so confused because my loving brother had explained that everything had been left to only him. The true heir of his father's empire and that he would still take good care of his stepsister as long as I was a good little girl. And I believed you!" She ran another hand through her hair. "Fuck, I should have listened to my mother!"

"Your mother was a fucking gold digger!" Aiden yelled in frustration.

In one fluid motion, Reagan jumped off the couch and took two strides toward her brother, slapping him across the face, leaving a streak of red across his cheek. "Don't you fucking dare talk about my mother!" She growled and started pacing the floor.

"When I was shown the proof of the doctored will, all I wanted to do was confront you with the truth." She whipped around and kneeled down before him. Her eyes narrowed as she looked into his green eyes. "Oh brother, I knew you were a greedy son of a bitch but I would have never, never thought you would stoop this low. You see, when I found out there was no way to rectify the doctoring of the will, Lucas came up with a brilliant plan." She stood and walked back to the couch giving Lucas a kiss on the mouth and then sat next to him.

"When Lucas explained that he knew you still wouldn't give me half of what they bought you out for, he offered me as part of the contract to convince me once and for all how low you would go. Of course, I laughed it off. He was fucking nuts to think you would do such a thing. I told him right then and there it wouldn't work because even though my brother was greedy, he wasn't a sick son of a bitch that would sell his sister in a business deal and get an extra million to take her virginity!" She paused for a breath. "Fuck was I wrong!"

"Honey, calm down." Lucas stroked her hair.

Aiden's hand came up pointing at the two of them. "How long has this been going on? You only just met Reagan a couple of months ago?"

"Reagan's mother introduced me when she was seventeen. We started our romantic relationship six months after the car accident when she was eighteen." Lucas smiled and then kissed Reagan's forehead. "She's the best thing that has ever happened to me."

Reagan couldn't help but laugh at the look on her brother's face. Complete dismay. She finally stood and walked to the mini bar, "Please fill him in on the juicy details."

Reagan poured herself a glass of water taking a quick glance at her brother. He deserved everything they had just done to him and more. Even though Aiden was truly her only family according to paper, Lucas was her rock and had been for the last fourteen months. If it wasn't for him, she didn't know where she would be.

CHAPTER 9

Lucas knelt and pushed his face up to Aiden's. In a low, menacing voice he said, "I've been waiting so long for this day Aiden. Over a fucking year. I could throw your lifeless body on the steps of the LA precinct right now and get away with it scot-free you sick fuck." Lucas growled giving him one last withering glare. "Funny thing is- your sister wouldn't let me. She thinks leaving you penniless is punishment enough, for which I highly disagree."

Lucas stood up and exhaled loudly staring at Aiden and wondered if the man had any regrets. He doubted it. This behavior was in his nature. A sick twisted man that didn't give a shit about anyone or anything but himself. At least Lucas felt at ease knowing this was over and that Reagan would be safe finally. He sat down and crossed a leg over the other getting comfortable.

"You see my father Rex, was deeply in love with Reagan's mother. He knew he couldn't have her because she was loyal and loved your father. When Carey came to my father and me a few months prior to their tragic accident, she knew something was wrong. She had no trust in you what so ever that you would take care of her daughter if anything happened to them. Even after your father, Sean, had assured that Reagan would be well taken care of. Unfortunately, Mr. Lynch didn't see his son's deviant behavior." Lucas paused shaking his head. "Love is so blind."

Aiden hissed at Lucas' words. "Fuck you."

Lucas ignored him, taking the glass that Reagan offered him and watched her take a seat next to him. "Carey was well aware that your father had changed his will to include Reagan. And I had shared that information with Reagan shortly after you totally blindsided the one person you were supposed to protect. But being the gracious person that Reagan is, she wanted to give you the benefit of the doubt. See what would happen."

Reagan took a sip from her glass while she stared at her brother from above the rim and then said, "We watched and while we waited, we fell in love."

"So you both knew for over a year and did nothing?" Aiden asked cocking an eyebrow.

"Yes, Aiden. It's called patience. Something you'll never acquire." Lucas winked. "We knew it was just a matter of time until you ran the business into the ground. Once you had accomplished that, it was up to my father and me to offer you a buyout deal you couldn't refuse."

Lucas stood and walked behind the couch. He reached down and massaged Reagan's shoulders and said, "But when you agreed to give Reagan as a gift and even offer her virginity to me, I was floored. Holy fuck!" He smiled and let out a chuckle. "When I told her, at first she didn't believe me. I think it was the shock of it all. Trying to accept the fact that her brother was a worthless piece of shit. But then she finally accepted it and agreed to follow through with the whole charade. Just to see how fucking pathetic you really were and if you would actually go through with it."

"Fuck you! You're the sick one dating and fucking a minor." He spat.

Reagan stood and placed a delicate hand on Lucas' arm. "May I?"

"Of course. Take the floor." He said sitting back down.

"Jesus, you're fucking ignorant for someone who was supposed to run our father's empire. I legally became a consenting adult when I turned eighteen."

"So last night was all an act?"

"Not all of it. I was still a virgin. Lucas has been very patient over the last year with me but I did agree to go through with the plan and allowed him to take me last night for the first time. I like it a little rough." She said.

"But he raped you, Reagan." The look of horror on his face was priceless. She couldn't believe he was trying to come across as the good guy. She let out a breath and palmed the back of her neck. "Are you fucking serious? He didn't rape me. It was all a very well prepared plan and the fact that you sat there in your room watching, egging it on and jerking off to it is sick. You're fucking scum!"

Aiden played with his hands and then looked back up to Reagan. "Listen, I'm at fault for what I did, but I didn't watch or jerk off. I don't know what the fuck you're talking about?"

Reagan looked over at Lucas and said, "I'm growing really tired of this." Lucas nodded and Reagan gave Frankie his cue. He pulled Aiden up by the scruff of his shirt and sat him in another chair where he handcuffed his arms to the back so he couldn't move. Then pulled out a remote from his pocket and hit the button. The flat screen before them sparked to life. Only white snow flashed before the screen.

"Do you want to hold yourself to those words Aiden?" She asked one more time. He didn't say a word and just glared at the screen in shock. A moment later they all watched a woman walk in.

Her long silky black hair flowed behind her back. She wore a black trench coat with six-inch black stilettos.

Reagan couldn't contain her grin as she watched the horror on her brother's face. "Who the fuck is she? What are you doing?"

"Let's play a game Aiden. You wanted to watch me get raped by Lucas. Get off on seeing me get hurt. How about we watch Lasinda have a little fun with you?"

CHAPTER 10

One Year Ago

*R*eagan woke from another nightmare, panting and trying to catch her breath. All she could see was her parent's car going over the mountainside cliff with their distorted faces looking through the glass for someone to save them. Her long blond hair was damp and strands stuck to the sides of her face. She willed herself to calm down by taking in deep soothing breaths just like Lucas had taught her.

She looked up to see Lucas asleep in the chair next to her bed. He looked so peaceful. The way his arm was stretched out toward her reminded her of the protection he vowed to her mother and Reagan. To always keep her safe and never leave her alone. She touched the top of her head feeling the goose egg that had grown considerably.

*E*arlier in the day, they had gone horseback riding. Her horse had gotten spooked and threw her off violently giving her a nice bump on the head. When Lucas had tried to get to her, he slipped and fell in the thick mud becoming filthy.

Reagan loved the thoroughbreds that Lucas had at his private estate that was situated just outside of La Jolla. During the week, this was her quality time with Lucas, while her brother thought she was away at college or with friends. She would always return home Friday mornings and put on her game face and pray that her nightmare would soon be over.

She eased herself off the bed and noticed how filthy Lucas still was. He obviously hadn't showered and his hair was matted with thick clumps of mud. She padded off and ran a bath for him. She sat on the edge of the tub, running her fingers in the water as it reached the right temperature when she heard him yell.

"Reagan! Reagan!"

She ran out of the bathroom to see him lurch toward the door to the hall. His eyes frantic.

"Lucas, I'm right here."

He jerked his head toward the sound of her voice. His long strides ate up the distance between them and then he took her face in his hands, kissing her mouth deeply. Reagan was surprised at how worried he was.

"Jesus, baby, when I woke up and you were gone, I thought something happened." The hitch in his voice revealed his concern and before she could decipher the crazy look in his eyes, he pulled her roughly into his arms.

"It's ok, Lucas. I'm ok," she murmured, sliding her hands up his back and leaning into him. As she rested her cheek on his chest, he hunched his shoulders and his hot breath drifted through her hair.

She pushed away and looked up at him. "I ran you a hot bath." She tried to run her fingers through his hair but they just caught and she laughed. "You need one pretty bad." She watched a smile creep to his lips as he kissed her again. "Come on big guy, in the tub you go." She told him as she turned the water off.

For a moment he just stood there, breathing deeply and staring at her. "What?" she asked smiling.

"My robe looks good on you."

She could see the possessiveness in his eyes and she loved it. Reagan was his and only his. For the last six months after she lost her parents, Lucas had been there for her night and day if she needed him. At first, he was only there to look out for her, but then it turned to lust and the attraction grew so strong she couldn't deny it any longer. When she had turned eighteen only a month ago, they both couldn't deny the chemistry that was there but he refused to have sexual intercourse with her considering he was eleven years older and even though she was a consenting adult.

She loved the respect he had for her and it only allowed them to grow closer. But there was certainly nothing stopping them from having a little fun experimenting.

"Come on. In you go." She said firmly.

"I don't usually take baths."

She cocked an eyebrow. "Well, today you are." Reagan didn't give him a chance to protest and proceeded to strip him, muttering how dirty he was. Seconds later he was naked, sliding into the hot water. A groan of pleasure escaped him as he submerged himself completely; the liquid heat surrounded him and he gradually let go of the rigid control that he normally wore like armor. After a few moments of indulging, Lucas sat up and Reagan was grinning at him. He gave her a wide smile. He couldn't remember the last time he felt this good without sex.

She grabbed the soap and started lathering up his chest when his hand came up and cradled hers, stopping the motion. "I can do it."

She got to her feet and stood there with her hip cocked. Her brows were drawn together in a frown and her arms were crossed like she was angry. "You're hopeless, Mr. Ferris." She said with a grin.

A strange lump rose in his throat. Her hazel eyes were like summertime, full of welcome and promise and youth. When he looked into them it felt like his dark indomitable heart felt like it was being bathed in the hope and sunshine of what was to come for the two of them.

He'd lived his life taking what he wanted from women according to his own strange sense of honor and he'd been satisfied. He had never once wished for a normal life of a love that most people had always sought out. Lucas had always known that wasn't for him but in the short amount of time being with Reagan...he knew she had changed that in him. He realized now how much he needed her in his life, and not just in his bed.

He suddenly felt overwhelmed, happy and hopeful of what was to come. The possibilities of marriage and children. His entire body ached as he pictured her curled up by the fire in his chalet, completely naked. My god, how he wanted that. To make her smile and be happy like she had always deserved. He sucked in a breath as reality hit him hard. Unfortunately, those thoughts would have to be tucked aside for now.

He had just told Reagan last week about her brother doctoring her father's will. At first, she was in disbelief; she refused the idea that her brother would go to that extreme. She had been so distraught over it. She loved Aiden like a blood brother and could not process that he would betray her like this. Lucas finally had no choice and told her about what her mother, Carey had felt.

"But why wouldn't she have told me her suspicions?" Reagan cried, clearly distressed.

Lucas grabbed her trembling hands and held them in his. "Reagan, she didn't want you to have to be concerned with any of this. That is why I came into your life. No one knew for sure if this is what he had planned on doing and she knew you loved Aiden like he was your blood. But now things have changed and I'm here to take on this burden with you, to make it right. I vowed to you and your mother that I would not allow him to hurt you or take what was rightfully yours and when I make a promise, I make damn well sure I follow through with it." He kissed the top of her head and from that moment on their bond had been sealed as though they were always meant to be with one another. Each being their purpose in life.

It took Reagan over a week to accept the situation. Lucas

could see how it turned her harder, made her skin a little tougher and then the following week she had come to Lucas asking, "What do we do?"

Lucas had explained that they had to be patient and wait for Aiden to make a mistake. They both knew he would eventually, however they just didn't know how long it would take and it killed Lucas that Reagan had to live under the same roof with the slimeball playing this game. Making her prance around in front of business associates as a distraction made Lucas want to take him out right then but Reagan had assured him she could handle herself.

And she did. She played her hand flawlessly.

CHAPTER 11

Six months had passed since Lucas had informed Reagan of how deviant her step-brother really was. As time had passed and she made him believe that she only had him to rely on, his true self, began to slowly evolve into the monster he had always kept hidden from her and the rest of their family.

She was so grateful that her mother had such great intuition and her hunch about Aiden or she would have been really fucked. But because of Carey, she met Lucas. Reagan wouldn't be left alone. Their relationship had slowly grown into such a strong bond that no one could break it. As Lucas had told her, 'Patience honey, he'll fuck up. It's just a matter of time.' And he was so right.

Aiden had slowly been making the worst deals to date. Buying up property deals in the millions that couldn't be developed and then having to sell them off for substantial losses. Spending more money than he could afford to. They knew that it wouldn't be much longer before Lucas and Rex approached him with a buyout deal that he couldn't refuse.

She tried to get Aiden out of her thoughts and instead thought about how much she was looking forward to this upcoming weekend. She had arranged to spend it with Lucas in Switzerland, although she had told her brother that she would be staying with girlfriends. She was packing the rest of her items to make sure everything was ready first thing in the morning. She turned when she heard the knock on her door and watched Aiden walk in. Confusion marred his face.

"What the fuck is this?" He growled cocking an eyebrow and taking a few strides across the room to stand before her.

Reagan placed the last dress in her suitcase and stood her ground. "I'm leaving for the weekend. Don't you remember?"

She watched him palm his face and then shake his head. "What am I going to do with you? Huh?" His hand reached down and poked through the clothing that was neatly placed in her weekend suitcase. "You have already been committed to other priorities this weekend, sis." His words came out like venom.

Reagan tried to control her hands that had begun to shake and quickly hid them behind her back. "What are you talking about?"

Aiden grabbed a strand of her hair and pulled it to his nose smelling her scent. "I promised Mr. Whithmore, you would spend the weekend with him and that is exactly what you will do."

Reagan stood there staring at her brother in shock. "Are you serious? He's at least eighty years old. I'm not some plaything you can just rent out whenever the fuck you feel it's necessary Aiden. I'm your goddamn sister!" She seethed as the words rolled off her tongue. His blue eyes flashed wickedly and all she saw were malevolent gems staring her down. She knew she had just pushed him over the edge with her defiance. But god damn it, she was getting sick of this.

His hand came up so fast she didn't even see it. His fingers gripped her throat as he backed her into the wall. Her hands came up grabbing at his but he was so much stronger than her. Reagan's head hit the wall with a hard thump. For only a second he stared her down before his other hand came up and slapped her hard across the face making her see white spots.

"Things are changing around here, sis." His words dragged out the word 'sis' like he didn't believe it. "If I ask you to prance your little slutty ass around during a business meeting, you will do it. If I ask you to entertain a business associate for the weekend, you will do it." He paused and released his grip around her neck, then cupped her chin, his face only mere inches from hers. "Reagan, baby, I love you. You're my little sister. I would never put you in harm's way but you know that this will benefit the family business. Our business," he emphasized and then kissed her on the lips. Aiden finally released her and started to walk away as Reagan tried to gain control over her shaking body. He looked over his shoulder and said, "I'll cancel this weekend. I'll tell him you're sick or something. This time you get off sis, but next time, I expect you to be fully compliant."

Reagan stared in disbelief as the door closed behind him and then she sunk to the floor pulling her knees into her chest. She refused to cry. He would not win god damn it! She touched her cheek that was now throbbing and a moment later stood up. She zipped up her suitcase and whispered the mantra, 'You're strong. You can do this. You will win.'

∽

*R*eagan arrived at the chatel a little before noon that Saturday. After settling in she made herself a hot chocolate and sat in the living room watching the flat screen until Lucas arrived. He had told her would be arriving a little late due to business. She had tried relentlessly to hide the light bruise that had formed on her right cheek with concealer but to no avail, you could still see it.

The door slammed shut and she watched Lucas stride across the wooden floor and envelope her in an overwhelming hug. He nuzzled his nose in the crook of her neck and whispered, "Fuck, I've missed you. I don't like that you're not with me throughout the week anymore." He released her grip so he could look at her. She tried to force a smile but instead hung her head and felt the tears start to well in her eyes.

Lucas lifted her chin gently with his finger and forced her to turn her head so he could see her cheek. She looked into his eyes and saw the two swirls of blue fury.

"Hey, I'm ok." She said in a soothing voice. "It was just a misunderstanding."

Lucas ran a hand through his hair taking a step back. "Like fuck, it's ok. I swear to god, I will kill that little fuck if he lays another hand on you!" Reagan rushed over to him and grabbed him by the waist pulling his chest against hers. "It's going to be over soon enough. He'll get what's coming to him," she said, standing on the tips of her toes to reach his mouth. She kissed him deeply, relishing in his warmth and she let go. "I need you, Lucas. I need you now."

Lucas frowned, looking down at her and then shook his head. "We said we would wait Reagan."

"I know we did, but I can't any longer." She replied, almost begging.

He cupped her face with his large hands. "You can Reagan and we will." He said in a stern voice. "Are you sure you're ok?"

"I'm fine, Lucas." She walked away and sat down on the couch.

"Let me go take a quick shower and then I promised you I would take you shopping." He smiled and walked up the spiral staircase to the second level.

She stared at the screen thinking of the last encounter they had shared. It was so intense that just thinking about it, she found it made her feel tingly. He had kissed her and caressed her out in the open and in broad daylight when they had set up a private picnic. Anyone could have seen them. She pictured the one man that had spotted them and then just sat there and watched Lucas bring her to orgasm. She couldn't help but picture the man getting hard as he listened to her gasps when Lucas went down on her. The thoughts excited her, magnifying the sensations that were flowing through her.

Reagan would have never thought that being watched would turn her on so much that she could openly, and loudly, enjoy being eaten out in public. When Lucas had mercilessly driven her, teased her to the point of begging him to lick her cunt, she had been unable to control her loud moans even though she knew that man was watching them and could hear her. The orgasm that followed was so intense she thought that she might have lost consciousness for a few minutes, because when she came to she was on her knees with Lucas fucking her mouth, like a madman. She had remembered the first time they had foreplay. It was terrifying. His huge throbbing cock had repeatedly cut off her breath. But she found out quickly that she had loved it to the point she had craved it. With Lucas, she found that a sexual part of her had bloomed and he was slowly nurturing that blossom. She savored the virile, male taste of him, the power she felt from his thrusts.

She shook her head snapping herself out of her own reverie just when she heard Lucas pad down the staircase. Jesus, get a grip girl.

CHAPTER 12

After three hours of shopping Reagan's feet were throbbing. She and Lucas sat on the patio of a quaint and colorful little coffee shop and bakery called Confiserie Beschle an der Aeshenvorstadt. She had no idea how to pronounce all of it, but her espresso was perfect and their pastries would be worth the extra work out.

"So have you given any more thought to my idea about Aiden?"

Lucas took a sip of his coffee before he sat it down and looked at her thoughtfully. She knew that he had thought about it but he just wasn't sure about it. He'd expressed his concerns that since Aiden was such a sick son of a bitch, it might backfire on them. "Have you considered the fact that the sick bastard will probably get off on it?"

"I have," she sighed. "Especially since Aiden was the one that offered me to you in the first place. That's pimping me out and it's horrible, but how low would he really go?" As sick as it made her wonder, she had to know for sure. Lucas had a plan that would leave him practically penniless and Reagan had to know for sure that he truly deserved it.

"Okay," Lucas replied, sadly. She suspected he was despondent because so far his instincts about Aiden had been spot-on. He was sure Aiden would agree to whatever he wanted, as long as there was enough money involved. "You work on the specifics of that and I'll work on the contract."

"Does it bother you? I mean, doing it that way for the first time?"

He looked thoughtful as he took another sip of his tea. Then his eyes locked with hers, "You know how much I crave you. I can't wait to finally be inside of you. It's going to be my own personal heaven, I'm sure. But the way you're talking about going about it...you know if it was just you and I you could have it wherever and however you want it. But the idea of him watching...It makes me sick."

She reached over and covered his hand with hers. "I know. It makes me sick too. But there's still a chance that only his heart is black and not his soul too. There's the possibility that he'll say no and I won't know until it's over either way."

Lucas turned his hand over and squeezed hers. His intense blue eyes bored into hers showing concern when he spoke. "I don't think there's even a chance of that. I think he's the devil himself. There are no limits to what he will do to get what he wants and he has no conscience about it either."

Reagan felt a shudder rip through her body at Lucas' tone. She knew, especially judging by the past six months, that he was probably right. But a shred of hope still tugged at her. She had grown up idolizing Aiden. How could a man that had known and supposedly loved her since she was just a little girl—even consider handing her over to be raped and toyed with by a man she wasn't supposed to really know? She couldn't let herself completely believe that he would agree to that. She especially didn't want to fathom the possibility that he would get off on watching it. But she could fathom it, somewhere deep inside, or she wouldn't even be engaged in formulating a 'test' for him to begin with. She wasn't an overly religious person, but every night she said a prayer that somehow, she and Lucas and even her mother were wrong. She could live with him being greedy and a poor businessman...but evil was an altogether different story.

Reagan reminded herself that this was their vacation and she was wasting way too much energy thinking about Aiden. She traced the lines in Lucas' hand and with a naughty little smile she whispered, "Did you say something about a hot tub on our balcony?"

Lucas's entire demeanor changed. He smiled back at her wickedly. "I did say that.

~

An hour later Reagan stepped out onto the enclosed balcony dressed in a white crocheted Kiini bathing suit. The small white triangles covered her breasts and the faint outline of her nipples could be seen through the thin fabric. The V-shaped bottoms rode high and accentuated her curvy hips and smooth thighs. Lucas was at the wet bar making them a drink and when he turned around and got a look at her he almost dropped the glasses in his hands.

"Jesus woman you're going to give me a heart attack one of these days."

Reagan laughed. "You like the new suit?"

Lucas swallowed. "Jesus, yes."

"Thank you," she said with a grin. "I like yours too."

Lucas had on a pair of blue swim trunks and he had pulled off his t-shirt before Reagan came out. He liked to work out. He didn't do it as much for the hard body as he did for the peace of mind it gave him. The hard body was a bonus though, he thought, when it made a sexy nineteen-year-old look at him like he was something she wanted to devour. Lucas handed her the club soda with lime that she had requested and asked, "Shall we?"

She took a sip of her drink and smiled, "Yes."

Lucas put his free hand on the small of her bare back as she stepped up onto the deck of the Jacuzzi. He used his hand to guide her onto the first step and then once she was in the water, he stepped in after her. Reagan took a seat on the bench that wrapped around the inside of the tub and Lucas settled in next to her. The warm water and bubbles felt wonderful and the soft aroma of lavender filled his senses as Reagan snuggled in next to him. He put his arm around her and for a minute they both just sat there relaxing, enjoying each other's company and forgetting they had a care in the world.

When Lucas finished his drink he set the glass down on the side of the tub. Reagan pulled away from him and stood up to reach over and set hers down. It was an innocent gesture but one that gave Lucas an almost instant tent in his shorts. Her suit wasn't transparent but her nipples had become erect from the cold and they were so clearly visible that he could even see the little bumps on her areolas. He licked his lips as he thought about sucking them into his mouth. And then his eyes moved down to the V between her sexy, long legs.

The suit had molded to her inner thighs once it got wet and was almost revealing every inch of her smooth, shaved pussy. She sat down the glass and then slipped back down into the water. Lucas wrapped his arm around her and pulled her up against him, then crushed his mouth down on hers for a long, passionate kiss. Her hard nipples were pressed into him and he kept pulling her in tighter as their tongues explored each other's mouths, loving the way they felt through the soft fabric, against his bare skin.

As they kissed he let his fingers find the string that was tied around her neck and pulled on it. He heard her suck in a breath when he found the other one and did the same thing. Once it was loose between them he reached up and pulled the small piece of fabric out and tossed it onto the deck. He pulled out of the kiss and looked into her eyes as she gasped and panted for breath as he began to caress one of her nipples.

She shuddered as he trailed his fingertips along the sides of her breasts and tugged on the erect buttons. When she felt his mouth on the turgid peaks she moaned and leaned back.

His mouth moved over her breasts sending streaks of fire through her veins.

He took his time, kissing every square inch of her body, slowly, tantalizingly, driving her mad with every stroke of his tongue.

She tried to touch him. Reagan longed to feel his throbbing cock in her hands. She wanted to swallow him whole and take his spurting fulfillment down deep in her throat but he wouldn't let her. When she reached for him, he drew away. When she asked him to let her suck him, he said no. He gave her everything of himself, using his body and softly murmured words, and took nothing back.

"Lay back into my arms." His voice was deep and commanding and she did exactly what he asked her to. He had one hand on her upper back and the other underneath her ass, squeezing those amazingly sexy cheeks. He held her there for a few seconds just taking in the sight of her incredible body. He took in the sight of her full breasts, large, dark-red nipples, flat stomach and the swatch of fabric that had been pushed to the side so that as she lay there now, one of her wet, swollen lips was exposed. She let out a little surprised squeal when he lifted her up out of the water and laid her back on the deck.

By the time he nudged her legs apart she was writhing beneath him, panting with need. He lowered his body until his face was nestled between her thighs.

"Oh my god, Lucas. Yes..."

He placed his entire mouth over the smooth mound and laved her with his tongue. Reagan's body quivered as he sucked at the baby soft skin of her inner thighs and tickled her lips with the slippery tip of his tongue. Her wetness flowed from her pussy, down between her cheeks. Lucas made soft noises as he licked her juices, drinking it, drowning in it.

"I love the taste of you, Reagan. I want to lick you for hours."

Her entire body vibrated with desire as he teased her, kissing her everywhere but the one place where she desperately wanted his mouth. She shifted her hips this way and that, seeking the contact, needing it. She was aroused to such a fever pitch that when he finally slipped his tongue between her wet lips and touched her clit, she lost it. He stayed with her until the orgasm waned, his tongue flat against her. He grunted against her steamy flesh and squeezed her thighs with his hands. When she came down, he quickly brought her up to peak again. And again.

Over and over he made her cum until she couldn't take anymore and she begged him to stop.

Raising his head, he smiled at her. The storm clouds in his eyes were gone. The tension that always lurked in the lines and creases of his face had dissolved. All that was left was a sort of calm essence, a distillation of Lucas. It was as if she could finally peer through the haziness and see only him.

As he slid up and took her limp body into his arms, Reagan sighed, exhausted and trembling. There was no mistaking it— Lucas loved her. His feelings came across loud and clear just the same. When he touched her, his fingers sent tendrils of emotion along her skin. His tender, selfless foreplay nurtured those tendrils until his love was woven into her very being, around her heart and inside it. She felt it with every breath, every pulse beat. And it seemed to soothe away all the self-loathing, the shame and the guilt that had settled inside her. This man loved her.

She felt at peace when she closed her eyes and let oblivion take her.

CHAPTER 13

When Lucas and Reagan got back from Switzerland she found each task that Aiden 'asked' her to do to be more distasteful and harder to get through. Thankfully he hadn't asked her to spend time alone with any of the clients again…yet, but she had noticed that something in the way he looked at her had changed. It was like he had suddenly realized sitting the appetizers out in front of his business interests was enough to reel them in…but not quite enough to keep them on the hook for a long period of time. Reagan would notice him watching her sometimes and she could almost see the wheels turning in his head. The idea of her own brother possibly selling her to someone was enough to make her stomach turn. If it hadn't been for her stolen moments with Lucas she would have lost her mind.

Every moment she had when Aiden wasn't hovering over her or having her break in on a meeting to give the old rich men something to ogle; she was plotting and planning herself. When she first presented the idea of Lucas telling Aiden that he wanted Reagan for twenty-four hours, he had balked. He had adamantly refused to do it. But each time they talked about the things Aidan expected from her and how each task leaned more toward blatantly prostituting her than the last, the more Lucas began to come around to the idea.

Lucas had opened her eyes to the fact that she loved to be dominated and as much as the idea of one of the practical strangers Aiden might give her to, raping her and taking her virginity, disgusted and frightened her…the idea of role playing the whole thing with Lucas turned her on. She would sometimes even lay in bed at night, thinking about it and using her fingers to bring herself to orgasm or she would talk to Lucas on the phone about it and as they planned out the specifics and they would suddenly go from planning Aiden's demise to full-blown, hot and heavy phone sex.

It was hot and Reagan loved it, and she found the patience the two of them had shown thus far to be withering by the day. She wanted to really be with Lucas, and see him whenever she wanted. She hated sneaking around and she hated that Aiden was in control of every part of her life.

It was a Tuesday night after Aiden had choreographed her 'accidentally' interrupting a meeting at the office between him and Lucas and Lucas' father Rex, when Lucas called her and said, "I'm meeting with Aiden for lunch tomorrow at the house. Dad and I finally settled with him on numbers but I told him I wanted to meet somewhere privately to discuss the 'bonus' he and I had been talking about."

Reagan was thoroughly depressed about the business. It was something her step-father had been so proud of and with good reason. He had built it from the ground up with the intentions of his children and grandchildren reaping the benefits of it for decades to come. By children, he had meant Reagan too and it warmed her heart to know that. But if the business had to be sold, she was happy that Lucas and his father would be her partner. They were both brilliant, good-hearted men and she knew they would help her take it to new heights.

Reagan sighed knowing it was almost over. She would soon know if Aiden was Satan himself or the brother she had always loved. Maybe he had just gotten caught up and taken things too far. What Lucas was about to propose would cause the heads of most brothers to explode. It might even send a 'normal' brother into a homicidal rage. Reagan wasn't worried about Lucas on the off chance that happened. She knew that he was more than capable of handling himself. She only prayed that Aiden went in that direction and not the other.

On Wednesday morning when she came down from her room for breakfast she found Aiden sitting in the breakfast nook sipping his coffee and reading the paper. He looked up at her as she came into the room and smiled…and then he ran his eyes over her body, slowly, like he was picturing her without the jeans and blouse she was wearing. Reagan turned her back to him to pour her coffee but she couldn't suppress the shudder from the chill that ran down her spine. She had caught Aiden looking at her like that once or twice before, but she had convinced herself those times that he was thinking of something else and she just happened to be in the way. The very idea that he was thinking of touching her or doing things to her made her want to vomit. Who is this man and how was he able to hide his true colors for so long?

By the time she had her coffee she had composed herself enough to take it over to the table and sit down across from her brother with a smile on her face.

"Good morning." She looked out the large window next to the table and said, "It's a gorgeous day out there."

"Yes, it is," Aiden smiled, drawing his tongue across his bottom lip. Reagan almost curled her lip in disgust, but she caught herself and held the smile. "Why don't you spend some time out in the gardens enjoying it?"

She took a sip of her coffee and tried to act surprised as she asked, "You don't need me at the office today?"

"I'm not going to the office today."

Reagan took in his business suit and tie and the briefcase he always carried to work sitting on the counter near the table and asked, "Oh, are you taking a day off?"

"No, and neither are you. I want you out of sight unless I call you, but don't go far in case I need you. I'm meeting with Lucas Ferris again, this time just him and me one on one. He requested this private meeting and I have a feeling he's about to offer me a deal I can't refuse."

"Oh, well that's good. What kind of deal is it?"

Aiden shot her a look of disdain. "It's complicated business stuff that you would never understand."

Reagan almost rolled her own eyes. Over the past year, Lucas had been schooling her in business and how to read and understand contracts. He never wanted her to be taken advantage of again the way that Aiden had taken advantage of her with his father's will. Besides, if their plan turned out the way Lucas knew it would and Reagan hoped that it wouldn't, she would be the one solely in charge of the family's business dealings.

"Okay," she nodded with what she hoped was a sweet, clueless smile. "It'll be nice to spend some time out in the sun today."

After breakfast, Reagan had changed into a pair of shorts and a t-shirt and headed out to the rose gardens at the back of the estate armed with her iPod, a big floppy hat and a pair of gloves. She went to the tool shed and took out a box of gardening tools and carried it all over to the path that would take her into the midst of what had always reminded her of something out of a fairy tale, the way the multi-colored rose bushes wound around the cobblestone path. She spent the first hour or so clipping and trimming and just about the time she took her first water break she realized that she could hear male voices. She glanced over toward the back of the mansion and saw that the sliding glass doors between the veranda and the main living room were open. The screen was closed and just beyond it, she could see a large, shapely silhouette framed inside of it. It was Lucas and just the sight of his shadow made her mouth water. He must have asked Aiden to open the glass doors or opened them himself so that Reagan could hear what was being said inside. Although she couldn't hear the words from where she stood, the pitch and the tone of their voices told her they were having some kind of disagreement. She wondered if Lucas had told him the plan and Aiden's voice was high and strained because it disgusted him. She hoped that was the case.

Leaving her things where they were she quietly made her

way back up toward the house. She stopped dead in her tracks when the cell phone Aiden insisted she carried everywhere in case he needed her, vibrated. Looking down at the face of it, she saw that he had sent her a text that said, "Go in the front door and put on that white bikini...quickly. Then pass through the main living room on your way to the pool. Do not put anything on over the suit."

She curled her lip. It didn't sound like Aiden was balking what Lucas was proposing. It sounded like he was promoting it. She took off the hat and gloves and left them at the edge of the veranda and went back around front. Lucas' bodyguard Frankie was at the front door. He winked at her as she passed and she smiled back at him. Frankie was the only living soul besides her and Lucas that knew about their last year together and what they had planned for today.

She went up and quickly put on the tiny bathing suit and then grabbed a fluffy white towel. She made her way down the stairs and as soon as she was close to the living room she heard her brother's voice, "Did I mention her tits are like..." What the fuck? She stepped into the living room and Lucas and Aiden both stopped talking. Aiden was smiling at her with a lustful grin that made her skin crawl. She forced a smile back at him and then she looked at Lucas. He was smiling as well, but his eyes were doing their best to replace the cold that had run through her veins at the sound of her brother talking about her tits.

She smiled warmly at Lucas and hurried on past desperately trying to hide the anger that was flowing through her veins. She stepped out the door onto the veranda where she had been only moments before and closed the screen door behind her. She walked in the direction of the pool, stopping as soon as she was out of sight. That's when she heard Aiden chuckle and say, "Three, no lower."

Reagan thought she had never heard anything so vile as the sound of her brother putting a price on her dignity. The greedy, sick bastard really meant to go through with it.

She heard Lucas counter, "One. Final offer."

Aiden then said something to the tune of, "Okay, but just a few minor conditions…" and by that time she was walking away, quickly. She barely made it to the pool house before closing the door and dropping down onto one of the chaise longues in shock. She wondered if it was odd that she didn't feel like crying, now that she had heard it from her brother's mouth and with her own ears. She simply felt numb at first and then after a few minutes it was like a fire had been smoldering inside of her and suddenly without warning it flared up and consumed her. She wasn't going to cry. She was going to use that fire and the strength her feelings for Lucas gave her and she was going to ruin that son of a bitch.

CHAPTER 14

Present Day

Aiden's eyes went from the television screen to the sexy, but scary looking woman standing a few feet in front of him. Once again he struggled with the cuffs that bound his hands behind his back but to no avail. His eyes were dark pools of emerald as he eyed Reagan and growled, "Stop this bullshit. You know that you would have nothing if it wasn't for me."

She put a hand on her hip and asked, "Nothing? Really? Don't you mean I would have had half of everything that my step-father worked for his entire life if it wasn't for you? You're a greedy son of a bitch, but you know what Aiden? I could have lived with that. What I can't live with is the fact that you're also a sick, twisted bastard. And to make it worse, I was your staunchest defender for so long."

He started to open his mouth and Lucas yelled, "Shut up and pay attention!"

With an almost defeated look, he closed his mouth and looked back at the television screen. Lucas pushed a button on the remote and an image of the study where their father used to take his business calls came into view. At first, it was quiet and still and all that could be seen was the antique oak desk that Aiden's father had imported from Italy decades ago and the shelf of books behind it. Then the sound of a door opening and closing could be heard, and a lock engaging.

Suddenly Aiden could be seen making his way to the chair behind the desk. He took a seat in the big leather chair and with a look on his face that made Reagan want to retch he picked up a remote and pressed a button. What he was watching couldn't be seen, but every word of it could be heard. She could hear herself screaming out Aiden's name, pleading with him to help her. She could hear Lucas' smooth voice telling her that her brother had agreed to this…helped set it up even. She could feel her breaths becoming ragged as she watched the look on Aiden's face on the screen. She had seen the video before but that didn't make it any less repulsive to watch now.

"Turn this off!" Aiden screamed as if he was in a position to demand anything.

"Shut up!" Lucas bellowed. He reached out to Reagan who immediately melded into him and he held her with her face pressed into his chest while Aiden watched his own demise take place up on the screen. She wondered if he was ashamed at all. She doubted it. He was only upset because he had gotten caught.

The next time he tried to look away Reagan gave a little nod to the dominatrix that she had chosen herself, hand-picking her out of almost a hundred candidates. Lasinda shed the trench coat where she stood. Underneath it, she was wearing a black, fishnet bodysuit, black crotchless corset, and black gloves…and those sexy, strappy shoes with the six-inch spiked heels. Her body was voluptuous and her skin flawless. She walked with cat-like grace over to Aiden and taking his head in between her hands she forced him to look at the screen.

"What the fuck? Who is this bitch?" His eyes were wide like a caged animal.

Reagan saw one of Lasinda's long, pointed, red fingernails dig into the side of her brothers face. Blood as red as her nails slowly oozed from the spot as Aiden cried out. "You crazy bitch! What the fuck are you doing?"

"My name is Mistress Lasinda and you will address me as such, or not at all."

"Fuck you!"

She let another fingernail pierce his skin and Aiden screamed. Lucas paused the film in front of them while Aiden swore and yelled and twisted, trying to get away. When he was finally exhausted into at least a temporary submission, Lucas hit the play button again and the screen was filled with the disgusting image of her brother unzipping his pants and taking out his throbbing hard cock. He had a sick smile on his face as he watched what he thought was his little sister's rape and he slowly manipulated his cock with his hand, getting more excited each time he had heard Reagan cry out for him to help her.

Lucas held her tighter and he was the only thing at that moment keeping her from picking up a letter opener off the desk and shoving it through one of Aiden's eyes and into his brain.

They forced him to watch the entire video and once Lucas switched it off, Mistress Lasinda let go of Aiden's face and he slowly turned to face his sister. He had tears streaming down his face mixing with the blood from the wounds the Mistress had inflicted. Reagan wasn't fooled into thinking they were tears of regret. What they were, were tears for himself and what he was about to lose because he was a filthy douche bag.

"Mistress Lasinda is going to have some fun with you now," Reagan furrowed her brows as she spat the words out at him. "It will go much easier for you if you don't resist."

"Reagan don't do this. This is crazy. You know I love you. I'm your brother…Please…"

Reagan couldn't hold back any longer. She walked over to Aiden and pulled her arm back, letting it go and slapping him so hard across the face that it made his head snap back. "Don't you ever call yourself my brother again. After today you will be nothing but a fucking memory to me, one I will live every day trying to shake." She looked at Lasinda and said, "Make him beg." A second later she stormed out of the room but waited at the door for Lucas. She heard him walk over to Aiden and say, "You signed for the sale of the company with all proceeds going to your sister, including the million-dollar bonus. So, once we finish our little game here, she and I will leave so you can begin to figure out what you're going to do for money after today."

"What the fuck are you talking about?"

"The contract...the one that gave me twenty-four hours to do what I liked to Reagan. You said you read it." In a feigned, shocked voice Lucas said, "Don't tell me that an astute businessman such as yourself signed something he didn't read."

"You fucker! It won't hold up in court. You won't get away with this."

"Oh, I think we will. But hey, take us to court. It'll be fun telling the judge how Reagan and I have been together for an entire year without your knowledge and how you thought you were selling your sister to a man that wanted to ravage and rape her and then walk away. Oh and showing him the tape of that sick smile on your face as you beat off watching the whole thing really sounds like fun too. So I guess we'll see you in court."

As Lucas walked toward Reagan, Aiden began to scream wildly. He sounded like a maniac, that was until Mistress Lasinda stuffed a ball gag in his mouth and cut off the sound. All they could hear as the door closed behind them were sobs and gasps. As soon as the door was shut Lucas slid his arm around Reagan and asked, "So, you're sure you don't want to watch?"

She shook her head and he looked relieved. "No. I thought I wanted to," she said. "I thought I wanted to be almost as sick as my brother so that I could get back at him for the things he did to me. But the truth is as much as I know he deserves everything she's about to dish out, I'm not sick enough that watching it would help with my revenge."

Lucas kissed her forehead and said, "You're not sick at all. He's the sick one. Let's get out of here."

Aiden was still trying to process what had just happened when Lucas' bodyguard Frankie walked into the room. The woman in black whispered something to him and with a sadistic grin Frankie walked over and unhooked the cuffs that held Aiden to the chair. For just a second Aiden breathed a sigh of relief, thinking he was going to be set free.

"Take him to the wine cellar."

Aiden was suddenly grabbed roughly by the arm and led out of the room. When he realized what was happening he tried to fight, but Frankie was too strong. He held onto him firmly and dragged him forcibly to the kitchen where the stairway to the wine cellar already stood open. He then practically pushed him down the stairs in the dark. Once they reached the bottom, the light came on and flooded the room. Aiden had known this cabin his entire life, but he didn't recognize the room he saw before him.

"Feel free to scream," the woman said in a husky whisper, "No one can hear you."

"This is fucking crazy…"

Frankie smacked him against the side of his head and growled, "Keep your mouth shut and listen."

The room went silent other than the tapping of the woman's heels against the cold, polished wood floor. The walls were paneled in dark wood and the racks of wine had been removed. The room was now filled with bizarre devices and what looked like torture furniture and all along one wall were neatly hung canes, whips, floggers, and crops. Aiden fancied himself somewhat a connoisseur of porn, so he recognized it all for what it was…but had he been into the BDSM scene, it would have been with him as the Dom.

He wasn't about to take this lying down.

Frankie practically carried him over to a large sofa against the far wall and tossed him down on it. He jumped back up and tried to run. Frankie caught him at the bottom of the stairs and forced him to turn around toward the couch. The woman was now sitting on it with her legs crossed. Frankie had Aiden's arms twisted up behind his back and he could feel sweat rolling down the side of his face.

This was fucked up.

Seriously fucked up.

He couldn't believe Reagan had any part in this. Did he ever know her at all? He guessed that was ironic, considering she had only recently figured him out. But that didn't make this any less fucked. He suddenly realized that there was no way Frankie was letting him out of here and he was at the mercy of this woman that looked almost ecstatic at the prospect of causing him pain. He swallowed the lump in his throat and tried to concentrate on what he was going to do to Reagan when he got out of there and got his hands on her.

CHAPTER 15

𝓕rankie held firmly onto Aiden and the woman on the couch began to speak, "Inside this room, you will call me nothing other than 'mistress'. You will not dare open your mouth unless you are asked to speak. You will obey instantly without a second thought. Do you understand?"

"I can pay you double whatever they're paying you..."

Frankie twisted his arm harder and he squealed in pain as the woman said, "You're making this much harder on yourself than it has to be. I will give you one more chance. Did you understand your instructions, yes or no?"

"Yes."

She sighed, got up and went over to the wall and selected what looked like a whip that jockey's used on their horses. Aiden's body tensed slightly as she walked up to him but even considering she might use the whip on him was nothing compared to the shock of the pain he felt as it made contact with his stomach. It was like a hot knife slashing into his skin. He screamed and began to sob. She stood in front of him, waiting. When he continued to cry, beg and grovel, she raised the whip again.

"I'm sorry!" He screamed.

"For what?"

"For not obeying," he said, breathlessly. "I'm sorry Mistress. Please don't hit me with that again."

She looked like she was considering it and then she whispered, "Since you're just learning I'll let it slide just this once."

"Thank you..." she raised a perfect eyebrow and he added, "Mistress."

"Good, now take off your clothes and fold them neatly. Don't try to run because Frankie will catch you and I will make you sorry. Do you understand?"

"Yes Mistress," he replied.

Frankie let go of him and as he fought through the pain and still tried to think of a way to escape, he removed his clothes a piece at a time and folded them.

When he finished she ordered, "Over in the corner there by the whips are some wrist and ankle cuffs. Put them on and bring the collar to me."

"Fuck."

The word was out of his mouth before he even realized it. She was behind him about two feet and the hot lash of the whip was so quick that he had never even felt it coming. He screamed as he moved toward the corner. Shaking, crying and breathing heavily he dug for the cuffs. As he put them on he had a visual of Lucas strapping Reagan to the bed and of himself holding his throbbing cock in his hand as he watched. Even now as he was trying to draw up some sympathy for someone else that wasn't there, his cock jumped at the vision of her being humiliated. He was glad at least that the dominatrix couldn't read his mind.

He started back toward her with the collar and she slapped the whip on the floor and snarled, "Crawl bitch."

With shaky limbs, Aiden dropped down to the cold floor and crawled over to where she stood. When he got there he sat back on his haunches and held the smooth leather collar studded with steel spikes, out to her.

She reached down and pet him with her hand like he was a dog and then she took the collar and strapped it around his neck...almost too tightly. She held out her hand and Frankie laid a long, leather leash in it. She attached that to the collar. Then she started walking toward another door that Aiden knew was a small bathroom. She pulled on his leash which tugged his collar and he was forced to either crawl after her or choke. He crawled like a dog and when she opened the door and turned on the lights he could see himself in the full-length mirror. He had never been so humiliated in his life...or so he thought. He heard a sound to his right and looked over to see Frankie, filming the whole thing.

"What the fuck are you going to do with that video?"

Instead of answering him Frankie looked at the mistress. "You do have a filthy mouth, my pet," she smirked. "We'll have to do something about that. But we'll save that for later. Remember what I said, do not speak without permission. Got it?"

"Yes Mistress," his voice sounded defeated. He wished that Reagan had stayed. He thought he could apologize to her and she would stop this. But if she wasn't even here...who knew how far this crazy bitch planned on taking it?

"Do you like the way you look on a leash and on your knees like the dog that you are?" she asked cocking an eyebrow.

"Yes Mistress," he lied.

"Good, because if you're going to act like an animal then you should be treated like one. You sold your own sister to the highest bidder. That's the most disgusting thing I've ever heard, and I've heard a lot. You have to be punished for that. You understand this is for your own good, right my pet?"

In a shaky voice, he said, "Yes Mistress."

"Good."

She took his leash and led him over to what looked like a wooden cross. "Face it and put your arms out." Aiden did as he was told and she roughly brought up one of his arms and clasped his wrist to a metal cuff attached to the cross. He resisted slightly as she attempted to clasp the other.

That was a mistake.

She beckoned Frankie over and while he nearly pulled Aiden's arm out of its socket fastening the second cuff, she gave him another lash on the back with the whip. He was trying not to cry out but it hurt so fucking bad. He was shaking and crying and it was so hard not to beg. He felt like a ten-year-old girl. He was terrified. That was when the look of terror Reagan had on her face when she first opened her eyes to Lucas molesting her crossed his mind. He still didn't feel sorrow, but he did feel nausea now.

He could hear the click of her heels as she paced back and forth behind him while Frankie secured his ankles to the floor. Once Frankie moved away he heard her walk around in front of him. She looked down at his crotch to his still soft cock and smirked. "Open your mouth," she spat.

As soon as he did she shoved a gag into it like the one she had used on him upstairs. He choked and gagged as she secured it behind his head. The ball kept his mouth from closing and he could feel drool running down his face. He looked up and saw that Frankie was looking amused as he filmed it all.

The mistress then put a blindfold over his eyes and cut his senses further. All he really had then was his hearing and touch. All he wanted to touch was the steering wheel of his Beamer as he got the hell out of there…but he knew that wasn't going to happen. He hung there listening to her pull something off the wall and braced himself for the first blow.

He heard the click of her heels as she walked toward him and suddenly he felt it. It was a splitting kind of pain that traveled from where she'd landed the blow on the cheeks of his ass all the way up to the top of his back. He screamed around the gag. If he could talk he would probably be in all sorts of trouble because, in his head, he was calling her every filthy name in the book. It was at least twenty lashes later when she asked, "Do you understand that you brought this all on yourself?"

He felt on the brink of unconsciousness but he was afraid that if he blacked out she might kill him. He nodded and she said, "Good. By the time we finish here you will understand that greed, arrogance, and perversion are not good qualities, especially in the confines of a family. When I finish with you, you will be ready to apologize to your sister and sincerely tell her what a piece of garbage you are. Do you understand?"

As she talked he could hear something slapping against her palm. It sounded heavier or thicker than the whip. He nodded again, hoping she wouldn't use whatever it was on him. She got close enough to him then that he could smell her and she reached up and removed his blindfold. What he saw in her hand sent a wave of terror through him, unlike anything he had ever felt before. It looked like a belt, but attached to it in the center was the biggest god damn dildo he had ever seen. It was at least nine or ten inches long and two inches in girth. He was glad for the gag because he would have asked her a question that got him in trouble without it. She took the gag out slowly, letting him see the marks his teeth had left on it as she pulled it away. Then she knelt and unhooked his ankles and said, "Get on your knees and lick my shoes while you thank me for your discipline."

That beat the hell out of thinking what the dildo was for, so he did what she asked. After she tired of watching him lick the leather and her feet around it, she ordered, "Stand up."

They both got to their feet and he saw her signal, Frankie. The big guy came and picked him up by the shoulders and carried him over to the sofa.

"Put your stomach against the back of it."

Aiden complied and suddenly panicked more than he had so far as he felt his ankles being bound. He tried to stand up but Frankie's beefy hand just kept pushing him back into the couch. Once his ankles were secured Frankie bound his arms and gave him another smile before stepping away. The next thing that filled Aiden's vision made him scream, and then beg, and grovel, and plead…and then cry.

The mistress was wearing the belt and that huge, fake cock protruded out from her groin. She smiled and purred, "Are you ready for your next lesson? Would you like to know first-hand what it feels like to be raped?"

"No Mistress. Please. I'm so sorry."

She smiled and actually leaned down and kissed him softly on the lips and then she hissed, "Hold onto something tight my pet…I'm about to take your cherry."

CHAPTER 16

One Year Later

"Are you nervous?"

Dad and Lucas had met at the Starbucks down the street from his and Reagan's new penthouse apartment for coffee the morning of the wedding. Reagan hadn't been home in two days and missing her was making him grouchy and borderline depressed. She was staying with her friend Belinda that she had met once she was free from her brother's stronghold on her. She was finally free to enjoy her life and as pleased as Lucas was to see her so happy, he still missed her every second they were apart. In his defense, these two days had been the first time they had been apart at night in a year. In her defense, today was her wedding and she needed time to do her girl stuff and get ready without him over her shoulder.

"Not really," Lucas told his father.

It was kind of true. He wasn't nervous about being married to Reagan, for that he couldn't wait. He was a little nervous about being a good husband and eventually a father. He wanted to give Reagan the world, the best of everything and sometimes he worried that he couldn't be what she deserved.

"She loves you son. I can see it in her eyes every time she looks at you."

Lucas smiled. "I know she loves me. I feel like the luckiest man in the world."

"You are," his dad smiled, "Not everyone gets a chance to even meet their soulmate much less spend the rest of their lives with them."

Lucas nodded. "I thank God for that every day, Dad. Can I ask you a question, though?"

"Of course."

"I know that Mom wasn't your soulmate. I know that because you loved Carey for so long. But you didn't cheat on Mom and I don't believe you would have even if Carey would have agreed to it. So, you must have loved her too, right?"

"Of course I did. I loved your mother very much. I met Carey when your mother and I were going through some hard times. Maybe that's why it was so easy for me to fall in love with her. Or maybe, she was my soulmate and I just met her too late. But whatever it was, I wouldn't have ever hurt your mother that way. She was an incredible woman and I wish she was still here to see you marry Reagan. She would have been so proud of you…of both of you."

A sad smiled marred Lucas' face. His mother's death had been hard on him, but his father had always been his rock and his presence in his life had helped him through it.

"I wish she was here too. I am so grateful that you are. It hurts that Reagan's parents didn't get to see her walk down the aisle. In case we haven't told you, we are so grateful to you for stepping up and offering to walk with her."

"Reagan has thanked me profusely too many times. I'm so happy and proud to do it."

Lucas sighed. "So, when you and Mom got married and started a family, were you ever worried that you wouldn't know what you were doing and you'd screw it all up?"

Rex smiled and took a sip of his coffee before saying, "Pretty much all the time."

"That's reassuring," Lucas laughed.

"Well, you're proof that I didn't screw it up too bad. Look, son, everyone wishes that marriage and parenthood came with a step-by-step manual, especially type 'A' personalities like you." He grinned at his son and went on, "But since they don't, all you can do is your best every day. The most important thing is love and as long as you have that you have everything you need."

"I hope so," Lucas agreed. "Reagan's finally recovering from what her brother did to her. All she's ever wanted was an intact family and I want more than anything to give that to her. I just want to do it right."

"I have faith that you will," Rex grinned. They drank their coffee in silence for a few minutes and then Rex asked, "Speaking of the devil, have you two had any more problems with him?"

"Not for a while," Lucas said. His father had hit on the biggest worry he had of all…Aiden Kade and what the crazy bastard might do next.

After the night that he and Reagan left Aiden with Mistress Lasinda for his 'punishment' things in their lives were chaotic, to say the least. The first three weeks were wonderful. They made love every day and night, more often than not in new places and they spent nearly every second making up for the time they lost with each other because of Aiden. They felt like they could finally breathe without his constant presence in their lives.

During that time, they had Reagan's things moved out of the mansion in La Jolla and into the family home that Lucas shared with his father. Lucas was sure Aiden would begin liquidating the assets he had left as soon as he got back and he wanted to be sure that Reagan had what she wanted before he did that. Reagan only wanted what was hers and a few boxes of photos and mementos that her mother had kept up in the attic. She had broken down at the fact he had nothing so she agreed to allow him to strip the house of what he wanted. This would give him a fresh start. Lucas didn't understand why she did it because the bastard didn't deserve anything but he knew deep down she still felt sorry for him. Reagan was just happy that she didn't have to live under that roof with a monster any longer.

Just as Lucas suspected, as soon as Aiden returned to La Jolla he almost immediately began selling off the family assets. He had three cars, a jaguar, an SUV and a BMW. He kept the BMW and sold the other two, and then he started on the antiques and art inside of the house. There were Persian rugs worth thousands and original paintings worth tens of thousands. Reagan had taken what she wanted of her mother's jewelry, but what was left probably brought in a cool million. Lucas couldn't help it, he was furious when he thought about how much money Aiden was making off of it all, but Reagan had easily calmed him down by telling him that it didn't matter because they had something that Aiden would never have…love, and each other. Lucas may have left it at that if Aiden hadn't turned to trying to harass Reagan. At least Lucas strongly suspected it was him. He just hadn't been able to prove it yet.

Once they were back in town and the new and revamped company was up and running, Reagan enrolled in college and went to work at their side within the company. He didn't believe there was anything that she couldn't do. She was smart and driven and besides, she owned the largest percentage of the company. But she insisted that she wanted to learn the business from the sidelines while she worked on her degree. It was hard for Lucas to take a step back and let her do it that way, but he had to respect her decision. It said a lot about her character and made him love her even more. Once she settled into her new job, however, that was when things began to go south.

First, the flowers began arriving. She would arrive at her desk in the morning and a vase of black roses with notes that said things like, 'The color of your soul.' and 'Hope your life is as bleak as these roses.' Lucas tracked down the delivery of each bouquet. Whoever bought them had used a different florist in the greater San Diego area each time and had always paid with cash. The description that the people who remembered him gave vaguely matched Aiden, but when shown a picture of him, no one could say for sure. The man that bought the flowers wore a hat and had what people described as 'several day's growth of beard on his face.'

Lucas beefed up the security at the company and had the deliveries stopped before they reached Reagan. There was a lull for a few weeks and then the letters began arriving at the house. Each letter was filled with vile gibberish and went on sometimes pages about what a 'gold-digging slut' Reagan was. There was no way to trace them since they were written with letters cut and pasted from magazines and mailed from different places throughout the city each time. Lucas wanted to go over and beat Aiden senseless with his bare hands but Reagan begged him not to do it. She was convinced that it was what Aiden wanted. It was probably all part of a plan where he could press assault or even attempted murder charges against Lucas and have him arrested. He wasn't going to take what happened to him at the cabin to court for fear of how it would make him look…but if Lucas assaulted him without any proof that he was the stalker, he would look like the victim. Lucas knew she was right, but damn it was hard not to want to kill him.

Instead, Lucas began having one of the staff go through the mail before Reagan saw it and taking out the letters. He also hired a security company to follow Aiden around and photograph everything he did. In the meantime, as they tried to get on with their lives, Lucas proposed. He had put a lot of thought into how he wanted to do it and finally settled on a way that he hoped Reagan would love. He thought about it now and smiled. All thoughts of Aiden were gone as soon as his mind went back to that day.

It was a Friday morning and Reagan was at her desk at work. She looked adorable he thought in a blue plaid skirt and white button-up cotton blouse with her silky blonde hair curled around her shoulders and looking like spun gold in the reflection of the fluorescent lights. It still amazed him how his heart practically stopped beating every time he saw her and then restarted and began to beat only for her.

"Hey, beautiful. It's time to call it a day."

Reagan smiled up at him from behind her desk. "It's only eleven a.m."

"Yep, and it's time to call it a day."

"But who's going to cover for me?"

"I already talked to Brandi in HR and she's sending one of the temps down. She should be here any minute."

"But..."

"Stop arguing with me woman or I'll throw you over my shoulder and carry you out of here like a caveman. She laughed and he said, "You think I won't? Don't test me, woman!"

Still laughing she got her things together and transferred her phone. Lucas had a car waiting for them out front and the car took them to a private strip of beach where they got out. Lucas took a picnic basket out of the trunk and he carried it in one hand and held Reagan's hand in the other. She had slipped off her shoes and she carried those as they made their way across the warm sand and to a pile of rock that overlooked both the beach and the ocean. They sat there and had their lunch, talking and laughing and looking out at the calming ocean. They both loved the beach and they had even talked about buying a beach house someday.

After lunch was over Lucas said, "Let's go for a walk."

Reagan easily agreed and he took her hand and led her further down the deserted beach. Reagan seemed to be enjoying the views and she was distracted by watching what she thought was a seal out in the ocean when Lucas stopped walking. She looked up at him and that was when she saw it out of the corner of her eye. Turning toward it, she saw a huge sandcastle. It was an actual castle with turrets, a moat and a big stone wall around it. It looked like it had been meticulously crafted out of the sand and Reagan just stood there looking at it in awe for a long time before she realized there was something written in the sand around the outside of it. She got closer and Lucas followed her. She felt like Dorothy in the wizard of Oz movie as she walked around the huge sandcastle and read what had been written in the sand.

It said, 'Reagan Kade, will you do me the honor of becoming my wife?' She looked up at Lucas's face and realized he wasn't there. He had gotten down on one knee behind her and in his hand, he held a white velvet box. He flipped it open and Reagan was nearly blinded by the sunlight that bounced off the ring of precious stones in his hand.

"I love you, Reagan."

She smiled through the tears that began to form in her eyes. "I love you too, Lucas, so much."

"Will you marry me?"

The tears fell one after the other down her cheeks. She wasn't able to control them and she didn't even bother wiping them out of her eyes before nodding enthusiastically and saying, "Yes Lucas! There's nothing in this world I would love more than to become your wife."

He slid the ring on her finger and then stood up. He wrapped his arms around her and pulled her in for a crushing hug. "You've just made me the happiest man on earth."

She looked up at him and smiled, "Good because I'm the happiest woman. We're going to have an incredible life together."

Lucas grinned down at her and nodded, "I don't doubt it."

After that they began planning their wedding and shopping for a home of their own, they looked at ten or twelve homes and finally settled on one they both loved as soon as they laid eyes on it. It sat right on the beach and the entire bottom floor was made of glass so they had views of blue ocean and white sands on all sides. It needed renovations but the contractor that Lucas hired assured him they could have it move-in ready by the time they were back from their honeymoon. As soon as they signed on the house, and were lulled into a false sense of security…that was when he struck again.

About three weeks into the renovations, Lucas' contractor called and told him they had shown up to the work site that morning and were greeted by a rotting, smelly pile of fish heads left in the center of the living room floor. As much as that infuriated Lucas, what made him even angrier was that Aiden wasn't anywhere near San Diego at the time. He had been working on developing a software company with some of the money he obtained by selling off the family assets and he was in the Silicon Valley. The security company following him had photos of him there for the entire week before the incident. Lucas was still sure it was him. He had simply hired someone to do the dirty work...but once again, he couldn't prove it. That was what finally put Lucas over the edge and for the first time and what he hoped would be the only time ever, he did something behind Reagan's back. As he thought about it, he actually smiled. That was a good day.

CHAPTER 17

Reagan stood in front of the full-length mirror in the bride's room at the Catamaran Resort and Spa. She had checked out the South Lawn where she and Lucas would be saying their vows in less than an hour, when she first arrived in the morning. It was set up with chairs for almost 200 guests and the long, white runner in between was offset by the multi-colored tropical flowers that lined it. At the front of it, all was a handmade bamboo arch decorated with the same type of fresh, fragrant flowers and sprigs of palm. It was a gorgeous, sunny day and the panoramic views of Mission Bay and the gorgeous blue San Diego skyline in the background topped it all off. Reagan had experienced more good times and happy days since she had met Lucas than any other time in her life, but she knew that today would be the happiest and most memorable. She couldn't wait to be his wife and start their lives together and although thoughts of Aiden and what he might be up to next kept trying to creep into her subconscious, she trampled them down every time. She had already allowed him to consume too much of her life. Today was Reagan and Lucas' day and there was no room in it for Aiden, even in her thoughts.

A knock on the door brought her out of her reverie. Before she went over to answer it, her friend Belinda stuck her head inside. "Hey beautiful, the makeup artists are here."

Reagan smiled. "Okay, I'm ready if you are."

Belinda was her maid of honor and she had been a life-saver. Reagan hadn't had any close friends since high school. Aiden had made sure of that as part of his attempt to control and dominate every aspect of her life. She had met Belinda at the company. She had worked for Rex Ferris for two years as a junior assistant and she and Reagan hit it off almost immediately. Belinda had also only been married for less than a year so she had tons of amazing tips to offer Reagan as she began planning her own wedding. Her husband was a really nice guy and although he and Lucas probably wouldn't ever be best friends because of their age difference, they got along well enough for the two couples to hang out and do things together on occasion. Reagan loved having a best friend and she confided almost everything to Belinda.

Belinda pulled the door open and two women and one man came inside. Each of them carried a leather bag full of supplies and they were set up and ready to work their magic in minutes. When they left the hair stylist showed up and by then it was time for Reagan and Belinda to put on their dresses. Reagan had worked with a designer from Bali who had created a dress for her that was beach casual but at the same time, wedding elegant. Belinda was wearing a pale green dress and Lucas, his father and his best man, a friend he'd had since college named Tim, were all wearing black tuxedos with light green cummerbunds and ties. The color wasn't Reagan's favorite, but it had been her mother Carey's. It was Reagan's way of honoring her and letting her know if she was out there watching somewhere, how much she missed her.

"So, are you nervous or excited or both?" Belinda asked her as they waited.

"Both," she said with a smile. "But you know what is consuming me right now more than nerves and excitement?"

"What?"

"I miss Lucas. I have barely slept in two days. I don't know how to sleep without him any longer. I miss him like someone cut off my arm and I had to live without it for two days before getting it sewn back on."

Belinda laughed. "Well, that's a good thing because you're going to be sleeping with him for the rest of your life."

Reagan could feel herself beaming from the inside out. The idea of being with Lucas for the rest of her life was a feeling that she couldn't even put into words if she had to…but the gist of it was all good.

"Okay ladies!" The wedding planner Reagan hired to help with the last-minute details barrelled into the room. She was so high energy that sometimes she made Reagan nervous, but she definitely got the job done. "You're up matron of honor."

Belinda gave Reagan a tight hug and whispered, "Good luck, honey. You look so beautiful."

"Thank you. Thank you for being here too."

"I wouldn't be anywhere else," she replied with a smile.

"Come on now before you make her cry and she ruins her make-up," the wedding planner nagged. Belinda laughed and followed the little hyperactive woman out the door. Almost as soon as they were gone Reagan heard the soft, beautiful harp music begin to play and she knew that her time to walk down the aisle was near. Another knock on the door produced Rex Ferris looking sharp and handsome in his tuxedo. As soon as he saw Reagan he let out a low whistle.

"You look so beautiful. My son is a lucky man."

Reagan smiled. "Thank you, Rex. But, I'm the lucky one."

"You're going to both have a great life." On 'life,' the wedding march began to play and the wedding planner was tapping on the door saying, "Let's go, bride, you're up!"

Reagan took the arm that Rex offered and together they stepped through the door. They stood at the start of the long, white runner and waited for their cue. Rex bent down and kissed her cheek and said, "That one was for your mama. I know she would have loved being here more than anything else."

Reagan's eyes filled with tears at the mention of Carey. The wedding planner appeared as if out of nowhere and handed her a tissue.

"Don't wipe, blot." Reagan giggled and gently blotted the tears. Then she took a deep breath and slid her hand back through Rex's arm. The guests all stood and Reagan and Rex began walking together toward the altar. She could see Lucas waiting for her and the butterflies in her belly took flight at the sight of him. He looked so gorgeous in his tuxedo and with an almost euphoric smile on his face. He locked eyes with Reagan and neither of them looked away until she and Rex reached the front. When they did Rex moved her thin, lacy veil out of the way and kissed her cheek before whispering, "I love you."

Reagan smiled and said, "I love you too. Thank you."

"No, thank you. Thank you for making my son happier than I've ever seen him."

He handed her over to Lucas and she slid her arm through his. Lucas was beaming at the sight of her. "God, you're gorgeous," he whispered.

"So are you," she winked. He looked so gorgeous as a matter of fact, she wanted to jump him right there. She was amazed at the fact that after two years together the sight of him still gave her goose bumps and caused her breath to catch in her throat.

"Are we ready to get started?" the minister asked them.

"Yes," they both said in unison.

Reagan was smiling so broadly that her face almost hurt. She didn't even care where Aiden was at or what he was doing. She was marrying the man of her dreams today and no matter what Aiden chose to do from here on out, he couldn't take her joy away. She couldn't wait to see what Lucas had planned for the honeymoon that he had insisted on planning in secret...And for the rest of their lives.

When they left the reception and headed for the airport Reagan asked a million questions about where they were going, but Lucas wouldn't even give her a hint, other than to tell her it was someplace she would love and a place where absolutely no one would bother them.

They flew on his company's private jet and Reagan continued to try and get out of him along the way where they were going. Lucas looked amused each time she guessed and held firm to not even giving her a clue. When the plane began to descend, she looked out the window and all she could see below them were snow-capped mountain ranges.

"Switzerland?" she said.

Lucas' lips quirked. "Nope."

"Wait! Oh my God! Lucas! What is that?" she asked excitedly, pointing to one of the snowy peaks. It was surrounded by very little earth and a lot of water.

He looked out the window and with a smile, he said, "That's a volcano."

"Lucas!" She threw her arms around him and he laughed. Reagan couldn't believe that he had done this. He had listened to her talk about her memories and realized how much they meant to her. It was just another reason why she loved him so much.

Once they got off the jet at the airport and boarded a small commercial boat that would take them out to an island, Reagan let her thoughts drift back to that weekend ten years before.

It was the weekend that had completely changed her relationship with her step-father and one of her fondest memories.

Reagan hadn't always adored her step-dad. When her mother first got married Reagan was overwhelmed by all of the changes and she resented him for taking precious time away from her and her mother. She felt like too many things were changing and in typical pre-adolescent style, Reagan decided to act out. She knew how proud her mother had always been of the good grades she got in school, so she started there. She stopped turning in assignments and studying for tests and by the end of her sixth-grade year, she was actually failing English, history and social studies and in jeopardy of being left back. Her teacher really liked her and she suspected that Reagan was just going through some hard times, so she gave her an extra-credit project and told her if she did well on it, she could make up enough of her grade to move on to middle school the next year. The assignment was to pick any town, city or island in the U.S. that she had never visited and learn as much about it as she could and hand in a comprehensive report on it the day after she got back from Memorial Day weekend.

Her parents did everything they could to encourage her and her step-father even told her that he would actually take her to visit the place she chose so that she could get a first-hand look at it as long as she promised to take the assignment seriously.

"Fine," her defiant little eleven-year-old self had said. "I want to do my report on Alaska."

Her parents had looked at each other and then her step-father asked, "What city in Alaska? Juneau? Anchorage?"

"Kiska Island," she said with a mischievous little smile.

Reagan had done her research. The island was an old WWII weather station. It was cold and deserted and it had an active volcano. She was sure her step-dad was going to say no way and it would give her one more reason to be angry with him.

Surprisingly, a day later their plane landed in Anchorage and they took a boat out to Kiska. In twenty-four hours her step-dad had arranged for a cozy little campsite to be set up for them and for the next three days the three of them explored the little island, collecting remnants from World War II and even climbing up to the top of the volcano. Reagan's most prized possessions to this day were lava rocks that she had collected that weekend and that trip turned out to be one of her fondest memories. It also cemented a bond between her and her step-father who after that trip she began to think of as her Dad.

∼

As Reagan and Lucas sat in front of a roaring fire later that evening in the brand new bungalow Lucas had built on the island, she was still at a loss for words.

"I just can't," she said as she sipped her hot chocolate. "I can't find the words to tell you how much this means to me." Lucas grinned and put down his mug. With a sexy smile, he said, "Maybe you can show me."

Reagan didn't waste any time putting her mug down too. They had both been holding back on the plane and the boat... waiting until the moment was just right. She stood up and went over and stood in front of him. He smiled up at her and said, "Are you ready to make love to your husband Mrs. Ferris, and then tomorrow we can go out exploring."

Instead of answering him with words Reagan took his hands in hers and brought them up to her chest. She placed them over her breasts and knew that he could feel her hard nipples. He began caressing them and she watched the desire on his face go from want to need in a matter of seconds. She loved having that kind of effect on him and more importantly, she loved that the feelings were mutual.

Reagan dropped down to her knees in front of him and reached out for his already throbbing cock. She ran her small hand across the outline of it in the front of his pants and the heat of it even through the fabric ignited the smoldering inferno in her belly. As she caressed him a sound came out of his throat that was something like a growl and there was instant wetness between her legs. He was so sexy that sometimes she wasn't sure she could stand it. She wanted him so badly, all the time.

He leaned forward, bending down and put his lips on her neck. She tipped her head back to open it up to him and he began to kiss and lick and then suck. She rubbed his now rock hard cock harder and faster as he took soft, erotic bites out of her sensitive flesh. She was gasping and her breathing was becoming shorter and more ragged. He was panting as he sucked and bit and the sound of it turned her on even more. The fact that he was so intense and demanding when they made love sent her into a sexual frenzy unlike anything she had ever felt and she hoped that she still felt that way after they had been married for twenty or thirty or even forty years. She never wanted to lose that feeling.

She suddenly realized that as he continued to feast on her neck, he was taking off her blouse. Once he had it unbuttoned and pushed back out of his way, his fingers slipped down inside her bra and found one of her rock hard nipples. He flicked it lightly and then took it between his fingers and began to twist and roll it, seeming to delight in the moans it was drawing out of her. She felt like her heart was going to explode every time he touched her like that. His lips slid up to her earlobe as he fondled her tits and he let his hot breath send goosebumps up and down her spine as he whispered sexy things in her ear. His hand went around from her breasts to the clasp on her bra and he unhooked it and freed them at last.

He looked down and let out another growl before pulling his head up and holding her back far enough to finish stripping the blouse and bra out of his way. Then he lowered his mouth and used his tongue to gently trace each one first, before clamping down hard around one and beginning to suck. Reagan felt like she was freefalling. It made her dizzy the way he heaped pleasure on her body. He wasn't just sucking and nibbling on her breasts, he was making love to them. She was on the verge of an orgasm as he moved from one to the other. Before Lucas no matter how much she fantasized about sex, she never imagined that it could be like this.

When he had his fill of her breasts…at least for the moment, he brought his lips up to cover hers and stood up, lifting her to her feet at the same time. He walked her backward down the short hall to their bedroom and gently pushed her down on the bed. The way he looked down at her with an almost predatory stare sent another convulsive shudder ripping through her. He reached down and pulled off the skirt she was wearing and then with a grasp and one twist of his big hand, he ripped off her panties and tossed the fabric aside.

Her body was burning up and she could feel the hair sticking to the sides of her face already as sweat trickled down from her brow. Lucas moved his hand up and brushed the loose tendrils back off of her face. That simple but intimate touch sent waves of emotion reverberating throughout her entire body. Lucas dropped down to his knees at the side of the bed and began to explore her body like he had never seen it before.

His lips kissed softly across her abdomen, while she ran her hands through his soft, tousled hair as he kissed her belly. She shivered when his lips moved down slowly toward the sensitive part of her inner thighs. He took his time, tasting the juices that had escaped from her wet pussy as she squirmed and moaned beneath his touch. When he sat up to pull off his own shirt, she could see the ripple of his hard muscle reflected off the sliver of moonlight that shone through the blinds that covered the little window. She had let her hands roam across his hard shoulders and chest and she marveled at the fact that he was all hers.

Lucas pushed her back so that she was lying flat on the bed and he moved on top of her. The searing heat coming from his body penetrated her skin and warmed her blood almost to the boiling point. He slid his tongue back into her mouth and as they kissed hard she ran her fingers over the muscular peaks of his back. She felt his hard cock pressing down against her thigh and she had never wanted anything so badly in her life as much as she wanted him to be inside of her, knowing that he was her husband now…and forever.

She felt his hand reach underneath her and begin to squeeze and knead at the cheeks of her ass. Her pussy was dying for attention, but he was making her wait and she knew the more she squirmed and begged for his touch, the longer he would make her suffer. It was always worth the wait, in the end, and then some…but tonight she had crossed the line between want and need already and she didn't want to wait any longer than she had to.

Lucas took his time caressing the round globes of her ass before sliding his hand around to the front and at last dipping his fingers into her slick, hot pussy. She moaned out loud as his fingers found her swollen bud and he began massaging it. She had her eyes almost closed but they were open enough that she could see the look on his face as he rubbed her clit. It was beyond intense. It was like he was incensed by the motion of her hips and the feel of her hot, wet pussy.

He suddenly started moving again and he pulled her to the edge of the bed so that her ass was right on the edge of it before dropping to his knees in front of her again.

He slid his tongue along her moist slit before opening her

lips with his fingers and shoving his tongue up inside of her as deeply as it would go. Reagan wrapped her fingers up in his hair and used it as leverage almost, to lift her hips up off the bed and meet those full, sexy lips. She was making soft noises as he licked and sucked and occasionally bit down on her clit and he didn't stop until she screamed out in an earth-shattering orgasm that rocked her to her very core.

Lucas never failed to reduce Reagan to a sex starved nymph that writhed and screamed under his touch…and she loved it.

"Please Lucas, I need you inside of me."

Reagan loved the feeling of Lucas' hard cock being shoved into her wet pussy right after she came when every nerve and blood vessel still stood at attention. Lucas smiled at her and stood up to finish stripping off the rest of his clothes. She reached for his throbbing cock again as soon as he had it uncovered and for a few seconds, he stood there with his eyes closed as she stroked it and licked around the head and down the shaft like it was a lollipop.

He pulled back and leaned over her and let her lick her own juices from his lips and face. The taste of herself on him was intoxicating and it drove her wild. His hand was between her legs again and his fingers were inside of her, but she needed more. She was dying for it. She put her hands behind his neck and pulled her mouth up to his ear and said, "I need you inside of me, Lucas…Please. Take me, fuck me, pound me, show me how lucky I am to be yours. Please let me feel you inside of me."

She felt him smile and then she almost blacked out from the sheer pleasure as he finally gave her what she wanted so badly, what she was sure she couldn't ever live without. He plunged himself into her deep and then slowly, almost agonizingly slow, he pulled out. He did it again and Reagan raked her nails across his back and wrapped her legs around his waist, trying to use her legs and feet to pull him in even deeper.

At first, it was frenetic with both of them desperate for what they wanted, but after a few seconds, they fell into a sexy rhythm that gained momentum with each one of his thrusts. Reagan was brought to climax two more times before she, at last, felt Lucas shudder and let out a primal groan before she felt his body tense, every muscle from head to toe…and then his whole body shuddered and he collapsed on top of her panting and quivering.

He lay there on top of her for a while before finally shifting his weight so that he wasn't crushing her and then wrapped her up so tightly that it was almost impossible to tell where his body ended and hers began. He kissed the side of her face and said in a ragged breath, "God, I love you." He turned her so that he could look into her eyes and whispered, "I have to tell you something and I hope that you're not angry with me."

Reagan felt a pang of worry. She didn't want to hear anything on this incredible day that would make her angry with him, but she also couldn't imagine what it could be. "Okay," she said simply and waited.

"I couldn't stand the idea of Aiden harassing us any longer."

With a shudder at the thought of what Aiden may have done, Reagan cautiously said, "Okay…"

"I sent him on a trip. He won't be back for a while…if he makes it back."

She pulled her head up so that she could see the rest of his face. "What kind of trip? Lucas, please tell me that you didn't do anything that could get you into trouble. I couldn't stand it if anyone took you away from me."

"No. I wanted to do something…permanent, to that slime ball. But I promised you that I wouldn't and I'll never break a promise to you. But I had an idea and I didn't want to bother you with it while we were planning the wedding. It was something I had to act on at a moment's notice however so I hope you'll forgive me for not running it past you first."

"I trust you," she replied, and she did. But her heart was still racing and her breaths were growing short. "Just tell me."

"Well, Aiden somehow ended up in the shipment of art that he sent to Europe."

"In the shipment?"

"Yeah…he's in a crate. But, he has enough food and fresh

water to last until it reaches its destination and an oxygen tank in case he needs it..."

Reagan felt her lips twitch as she tried to keep a straight face. "A crate?"

Lucas looked like he was trying not to smile as well. "My security people caught him paying off the guy that left the fishheads in our new home. He was down at the docks and they called me. I won't say that I didn't get in a few good blows, but before I killed him...while he was only rendered unconscious, I slipped him into one of the crates. The men and I had to act fast to get him all setup and once he was 'comfortable,' we screwed it shut. He should be arriving in the Congo in about a week."

Reagan lost her battle with the smile and suddenly had the giggles. "The Congo?"

"Yeah. I hope it will take him a while to get out of there and get back. That way we at least have a reprieve if he doesn't follow through on the promises he made while I was pummeling him with my fists."

Still smiling Reagan asked, "And what promises were those?"

"He said that he would pack up his things and move out of the state. He thought he might go to New York. I thought that was a great idea...but I wanted him to have some time to think about what the alternatives might be if he chose to stay around and continue harassing you, us."

"So you sent him to the Congo?" Peals of laughter erupted from her chest as she thought about her brother waking up on a ship headed for a remote and almost primitive place. She almost wished that she had a picture of it.

"Are you mad?" Lucas asked with a grin.

Reagan put her arms back around him and kissed him deeply. When they came up for air she growled in a sexy voice, "Just mad about you baby."

Lucas smiled, "I won't keep anything else from you ever again."

"Good," she said, "but while we're being honest with one another there is something I need to tell you. This morning before I left Belinda's house I took a pregnancy test. I haven't had my period in two months and I've been waking up feeling slightly nauseated."

"Oh, baby! Why didn't you tell me? We should have taken you to the doctor…"

"Lucas, I'm not sick. I'm pregnant."

There was dead silence in the cabin for what seemed like an eternity before a slow smile began to spread across Lucas' face. At last, he whispered, "I'm going to be a dad?"

Regan smiled back and nodded. "Are you okay with that?"

Lucas grinned back at her, "Are you serious. I'm thrilled." He pulled her into an embrace and smiled. "A baby."

One thing Reagan knew for sure was that things were changing, again. But she had come a long way from where she was and she knew that she could not only handle the changes, she was ready to embrace them. Her life as Mrs. Lucas Ferris was going to be amazing and even if Aiden wasn't smart enough to keep his distance when he showed back up, there was nothing he could do to take away the happiness she felt with Lucas. That dark and frightening part of her life was over and she was definitely on to bigger and better things.

WANT MORE? READ THE TEACHER & THE VIRGIN

An older man, a younger woman, an irresistible attraction.

TEACHER & THE VIRGIN - CHAPTER ONE

Jane

"*Who?*" the note read.

I turned my head to the right and met my friend Anne's curious green eyes. She raised an eyebrow up at me, remaining quiet. There was no talking in class, but I immediately knew what she was asking. Words weren't needed. Not for this.

Who was I planning to lose my virginity to?

Anne and I, and eight other girls in the senior class, made a pact to lose our virginity by the end of summer. Graduation was next week, so we had a couple months to get the deed done before we all went off to college. All of us being eighteen, we'd felt it was past time, especially since going to an all girls' school made near impossible to find worthy boys. We wanted to go to college *experienced*.

I didn't want to be the last virgin in our group, but I didn't have to worry. I didn't have to find a *boy* I liked. I didn't have to pretend to be in love, or chase after some stranger at the mall. I knew *exactly* who I wanted to get naked with.

I wanted Mr. Parker to take my virginity. I wanted my teacher to punch my V card.

Mr. Parker. He was only a few years older than me, and not skinny and awkward like the guys my age. No, he was *all* man.

While I saw him every day for my US government class, I doubted he noticed me. I was just one of his many students. One more young woman in an endless see of long hair and cherry flavored lip gloss. I existed in an ocean of khaki and plaid, the school's overly conservative uniform. Underneath, I wore a lace bra and matching g-string panties every other day, the days I had Mr. Parker's class.

And before class, I went to the ladies room and took off the bra. I loved the way my heavy cotton shirt rubbed my sensitive nipples, and I hoped he'd notice the hard tips that ached for his touch.

He was gorgeous and educated, his hard ass and broad shoulders made my innocent body squirm. I didn't want to be innocent, not when I was around him. I wanted to be naughty, but I doubted he noticed me.

But I noticed him. Every inch of his well-muscled form.

Yeah, he was the one who I was going to give myself to. I had no idea how, but it was going to happen.

He was gorgeous, dark hair that was overly long for the rules of the private school. He wore a tie to please the principal, but the knot was always loose, as if he hadn't the time to get completely dressed. I spent most of the class fantasizing about all the ways he could tie me up with that long strand of silk and turn me into a real woman.

"Ladies, I know it's the last day of classes before exams, so we're going to do a review on everything the final exam will cover. Colleges still look at final grades." His deep voice made me shiver and I couldn't stop staring at the muscles in his neck. I wanted to taste him. Which was weird, but I couldn't stop imagining kissing him...all over.

I wasn't worried about the final exam. This was the one class I was getting an A in, the one class where I always paid attention. How could I not stare at Mr. Parker for the entire hour? If the other girls thought I was gawking at the hot teacher, what did I care? They gawked, too. I couldn't keep her eyes of the flexing muscles in his forearms. He rolled up the sleeves of his dress shirts to write on the board, and I always had to go back and read what he wrote after. I couldn't stop staring at his hands.

Even Molly seemed hypnotized when he moved, and I was pretty sure she was a lesbian.

He was *that* hot. But none of the other girls would have him. No. If he was going to have one of us, if he was going to take a young, virgin pussy, then it was going to be mine.

I spent the entire year watching his ass as he walked back and forth lecturing. I studied the veins in the back of his hand as he wrote on the board. I studied his mouth and wondered what his lips would feel like against mine.

When the bell rang at the end of every class, I left the room with wet panties and hard nipples.

His class was the best part of my day. I even raised my hand to answer questions and preened when he smiled at me when I gave the correct answer. I wanted to please him, which was another odd sensation for me. I wasn't a people-pleaser. But for Mr. Parker? Well, I wasn't quite sure where I would draw the line, but I wanted to find out.

With Anne's note in my hand, I stared up at Mr. Parker from my seat in the third row. He was trying to be stern, but he was probably just as ready to be done for the summer as we were. The school was small, one of those girls' prep schools for rich parents who wanted a sheltered education for their privileged daughters. Yes, we always got teased about the usual stereotype, how we were crazy, spoiled, entitled brats with issues. The school had kept me from boys my age, which is what my parents wanted, but their plan backfired. It put me in front of the one man I craved.

Yes, I wanted a man.

I didn't want to be fucked by a boy who had no clue what he was doing. I wanted Mr. Parker.

Oh yes. I shifted in my chair, trying to ease the ache in my pussy at the thought of him filling me up. I wanted him to take my cherry, to split me wide open—his cock would be big—and he'd do it right.

While he continued to talk about the three branches of government, his smooth velvety voice only made dark carnal thoughts, wild fantasies, fill my mind.

"Fuck me," I'd tell him, glancing at the desk just behind him.

Yes, the desk. I fantasized about that desk almost as much as I did Mr. Parker. I was no longer the good student, but one who'd been bad. Very bad.

I'd be bent over his hard desk with my plaid uniform skirt barely hiding my ass. I'd have had to undo the top few buttons of my prim white shirt so he could see that I wasn't wearing a bra, my nipples tightening as they touched the cold wood.

A shiver would run down my spine when his finger grazed my lace panties. I would feel the heat pool there, making the damp fabric cling to my folds.

"You've been a naughty girl, haven't you?" the familiar velvety voice would say. His breath would warm my neck as he leaned over me, dominating me. I'd squeeze my legs together to try and ease the growing ache, but it wouldn't work. The press of his hand against the lips of my pussy would have me crying out.

"You're just wearing a thong in my class and no bra." His voice would be a mix of shock and mischief, and I would no doubt blush as he reached around and cupped an exposed breast.

Teachers weren't supposed to behave this way, I'd think, even as his other hand would come down on my ass in a harsh swat. They weren't supposed to reprimand naughty schoolgirls over their desks, but I would wiggle my hips because I'd want the spanking he'd give. I'd push my pert bottom out for more, for anything he'd give me.

"Do you know what happens to girls when they're naughty?" he'd ask.

"They get punished."

"That's right," he breathed against my neck. "But you're extra naughty, so you'll get my hand instead of the ruler. I want to make sure I can feel every single count."

Nothing about the way Mr. Parker would look at me would be soft. He would be like a beast with its prey. His look would be hungry, with me the answer to quenching his thirst. I would shiver again when his finger started to rub painfully, slowly against the gusset of my thong. His other hand would start to move against my ass cheeks, my bare flesh available for him.

"After your ass is nice and red, then you'll show me that you're a good girl again and suck my cock. Nice and deep." He would rub a finger over me, slip the tip just inside my virgin heat as he held me in place over his desk. "And then I'm going to taste your naughty pussy and make you come."

I moaned at the thought of him teaching me exactly how he liked it, of him dominating me, making me his. The mangled sound stirred me from my fantasy. I shifted in my seat again, trying to rub my thighs against my swollen clit.

All around me were my classmates, but they seemed not to notice the sound I'd made just *thinking* about Mr. Parker.

While he was the Civics and Government teacher in this small, private school, he'd finished law school last year and was studying for the bar exam. Being a teacher wasn't his career, like the other teachers who'd been at the school for decades. He was on the fast track to becoming a lawyer. He should have been stiff and stodgy; all the teachers were. Safe even, but nothing about the way he stared at me spelled "safe."

Sometimes, I imagined that he stared, that his gaze traced the curve of my leg or lingered on my lips. I dreamed that he wanted me, masturbated in his shower thinking about taking me over his desk. I dreamed that he couldn't control himself when it came to me, that I was so beautiful, so perfect that he couldn't say no.

No imagination needed on my end. I definitely wouldn't say no.

Mr. Parker was nine years older than I was – *yes, I stalked him* – and a man of that age had years of experience I could only dream about. That easily spelled trouble for me, but I wasn't running away from it. I wanted him and if I had to be punished because of it, I was fine with that, as long as Mr. Parker was doing the punishing.

Anne was writing something down on a piece of paper while the others worked on a practice test and whispered about what they were doing over the summer. I couldn't care less.

Why would I, when the only thing I wanted was standing right in front of me?

I spun around when another piece of paper hit my head. Anne raised and lowered her eyebrows at me. I realized my imagination had run wild again. I should've known better. Having almost-sex with Mr. Parker would *never* happen in real life. I saw him every day in class, and he'd never want anything to do with me. I was his student and too young. Yes, I was eighteen, but still...

The whole situation was hopeless. A man like him wanted a woman, not a girl. He would want woman who was experienced and worldly and didn't look like a lost puppy with a leash around its neck. I tried to brush the thought aside. It made me sad because I couldn't be alluring and experienced unless I fucked someone else and the only one I wanted was him.

I tried as best as I could to not think about it anymore, as I smoothed out the paper Anne had thrown.

"You're undressing our teacher with your eyes. Don't deny."

"Shut up". I quickly scribbled down before I passed the note back to Anne. She passed it back seconds later.

"Mr. Parker's too old."

I bit my bottom lip. That was exactly why he was so attractive; I got hot for an older man. I got hot for *him* and I quickly wrote my thoughts down.

"I bet he knows what to do with his c—"

I hesitated writing the last word. I was getting wet just thinking about writing a fucking four-letter word. It shouldn't have been a big deal – writing down the word "cock". What was I getting so worked up over? My classmates reading the note? Or worse, Mr. Parker?

Cock. Cock. Cock.

Cock. Cock. Cock.

See, I could say the word in my mind over and over again. Why couldn't I just write the damn thing down?

Cock. Cock. Cock.

Oh, God. My tongue definitely needed to be drowned in holy water.

"I bet he knows what to do with his cock." I quickly passed the note, letting out a sigh of relief that I finally wrote the damn word down.

Jane – 1. Cock – 0.

"You're crazy. He's a teacher. You'll be a virgin forever. He'll never touch you."

I pursed my lips when I read Anne's note. I didn't want to admit it, but the note stung, especially since I'd graduate next week and never see him again. It hurt because it was true. There was no way someone as gorgeous, smart, and experienced as Mr. Parker would want anything to do with an eighteen-year old Catholic school girl whose only sexual experience was with her own hand. I really was a virgin in all aspects, and the cold, harsh truth started to sink in.

How was I going to lose my virginity if I didn't know the first thing about sex? Sure, I knew how to pleasure myself and some porn videos seemed easy enough to follow, but would the real thing be as easy to do? The only dicks I'd seen in person were my cousins' back when our parents would make us swim naked together when we were four years old. I was a cold, lonely —and horny—virgin.

"We graduate in a week." I passed the note to Anne, bit my lip.

Now, I was just writing down random things in the hopes that she wouldn't see right through me and realize how affected I was by what she'd just said.

"He'll never touch you."

It stung, really. I'd been crushing hard on Mr. Parker since the start of the school year and now it was almost over. What would I do when I couldn't see him every day?

"He's hot."

"You ARE crazy. There's no way you're having sex with a teacher."

My reply to her was easy, and the truth. *"I don't want anyone else. He's the one who's going to take my virginity."*

Making it happen was impossible.

My jaw dropped to the floor when I saw Mr. Parker walking towards me. *Was my deepest fantasy finally coming true?* Of course not. Before I knew it, he took the notes in my hands and skimmed through them.

Oh. My. God.

I glanced at Anne and her cheeks were as red as her hair. She hadn't been the one who'd written all those things in the notes. She wasn't the one who was going to be in trouble. I was.

This was the perfect time for the floor to open and swallow me whole. This would be social suicide – my classmates finding out I wanted to fuck my teacher. Telling Anne in a note was one thing, but this? God, I'd never live it down.

I didn't even want to think about what my parents would say when I was sent to the office. They were absent most, if not all the time, and only seemed to care when it was to reprimand or ground me. I spent about half the school year living with the maid as they travelled Europe, or Africa, or wherever the hell they were now. Knowing I wanted to have sex with a teacher would make them freak.

I closed my eyes and waited for him to read it aloud like he usually did when he caught us passing notes.

Holding my breath, I looked up at him through my lashes.

His dark eyes were pinned to mine as he read the note. "Can't wait to be done with school. No more uniforms," he said, his voice loud for all to hear as he walked back to the front of the room.

I whipped my head up when those words came out of his mouth. He read it, knew the truth and didn't give me away?

I was safe from my classmates, but not from him. The way he looked at me curiously was a dead giveaway. I couldn't read him though, and it was freaking me out and exciting me at the same time. He knew how much I wanted him now. He *knew!* But he looked emotionless. Was he disgusted or infuriated? Was he even shocked, or was this a common occurrence with his students? Would he send me to the principal's office? Did he think the note was a joke? Or worse? Did he think it was real and just had absolutely no interest? Maybe he had a smoking hot model for a girlfriend, someone who knew her way around his cock, who knew how to please him.

I didn't know anything about what to do with a man. All I knew was I wanted him.

He raised his brow, and the blush that surfaced on my cheeks was automatic. Thankfully, the bell rang, and Anne and I stood up from our seats in a rush. I grabbed Anne by the arm and almost ran towards the door. I was almost free from further humiliation until I heard my name being called.

"Jane," said that ever-familiar voice that haunted my imagination. When my friend stopped to stand beside me, he added, "You can go ahead, Anne. I just want to have a word with Jane."

The rest of my classmates filed out of the room and Anne followed suit. When it was finally just the two of us, I clasped my hands together and waited for the sermon. I wanted to hug myself. No good could come out of my teacher reading a note basically saying I wanted him to fuck me. Was thinking dirty thoughts enough for disciplinary action? Could I be expelled? My heart sunk. Graduation was next week. There was no way—

He crossed his arms over his broad chest. "I want you right here, one hour after graduation."

I didn't want to overthink more than what I was already doing, but the way he looked at me made it seem that I had nothing to worry about. Instead, I had *everything* to worry about. I waited for him to say something more and watched as his eyes trailed from my ankle socks, up to my plaid skirt to my white blouse, then finally met my surprised gaze.

Did he know I was wet for him? Could he see me squirming from his scrutiny?

I never got the answer to that. When an unfamiliar student entered the room, that was my cue to leave and head to my next class.

"Jane, you didn't answer me," he said.

"Yes," I replied, starting toward the door.

"Yes, *sir*," he added and I stopped in my tracks.

A shiver coursed through me at the deep tone of his voice.

I glanced back, saw that he was waiting for me to repeat it.

"Yes, sir," I whispered, finding saying those two words really hot. Yes, I wanted him to be my teacher in more than just US government.

As I walked the hallways I'd never see again in a week's time, all I could think about was after graduation. He'd told—no, commanded—me to come back and meet him. I just had to wonder... why?

Get Teacher & The Virgin now!

GET A FREE BOOK!

Join my mailing list to be the first to know of new releases, free books, special prices and other author giveaways.

http://freehotcontemporary.com

ALSO BY JESSA JAMES

Bad Boy Billionaires
Lip Service
Rock Me
Lumberjacked
Baby Daddy

The Virgin Pact
The Teacher and the Virgin
His Virgin Nanny
His Dirty Virgin

Club V
Unravel
Undone
Uncover

Beg Me
Valentine Ever After

ABOUT THE AUTHOR

Jessa James grew up on the East Coast but always suffered a severe case of wanderlust. She's lived in six states, had a variety of jobs and always comes back to her first true love – writing. Jessa works full time as a writer, eats too much dark chocolate, has an iced-coffee and Cheetos addiction, and can't get enough of sexy alpha males who know exactly what they want – and aren't afraid to say it. Dominant, alpha-male insta-luv is her favorite to read (and write).

Sign up HERE for Jessa's Newsletter:

http://jessajamesauthor.com/mailing-list/

www.ingramcontent.com/pod-product-compliance
Lightning Source LLC
LaVergne TN
LVHW011843060526
838200LV00054B/4141